SANDS OF DOOM

JETHRO WEGENER

SEVEREDPRESS

SANDS OF DOOM

ISBN: 978-1-922861-22-1

CHAPTER 1

Rub' al Khali, Saudi Arabia, 1933

The thing that stumbled out of the desert and into the firelight of the Bedouin camp was only barely recognisable as human. It was unimaginably thin and ghastly pale, with sallow, sunken cheeks and ribs that poked out through tattered clothing.

But the creature's eyes were the most frightening thing to the men around the fire. They were wide, bloodshot, and darted crazily this way and that. They saw everything and nothing at the same time, their gaze enough to send chills down the spine of even the most hardened of men.

The man collapsed near the fire in a babbling heap. For a moment, the tribesmen just stared in open-mouthed horror at the thing in front of them. It kicked and twitched at odd intervals, sending waves of sand flying up into the night air.

It spoke in Arabic, although even to the native speakers present the words only barely made sense. The man's speech was jumbled and erratic, consisting of strange proclamations of doom and ear-splitting shrieks of pure, unadulterated terror.

The tribesmen stared out into the darkness of the desert surrounding them, straining their eyes to see what could have frightened their unexpected visitor so. Nothing moved in the blackness. The only sound that carried over to their ears was the odd grunt or shout of a camel. Yet none of them could shake the feeling that there was *something* out there.

Eventually, the leader of the group began to issue orders to his fellows. They gathered up the jabbering wreck that had once been a man, and wrapped him as best they could. The best marksman of the group grabbed his rifle – an aging Lee Enfield bolt action – and took up watch.

An uneasy feeling had fallen over everyone present, a feeling of terror that started deep within their guts. It was a feeling that many of them were unfamiliar with, having spent their lives wandering the desert sands with very little in the way of security available to them. Fear was not entirely alien, but it was rarely felt.

Every man present was feeling it then. The desert was their home. A place that they knew better than any other. It provided them with food and camel milk and water when they needed it. But at that moment, the land that they knew so well felt alien and strange. As if the darkness around them hid dangers that they had only just discovered.

One of the tribesmen was doing his best to hush the jabbering figure. To calm him down in some way. It was a futile endeavour. The figure did not feel safe, even among so many other armed men. It kept trying to tell its bizarre tale, even though the man found it incredibly difficult to form coherent words or sentences.

A sudden wind blew across the sands. Its touch was as cold as ice, sending goose pimples crawling across the arms of everyone around the fire. The fire itself flickered, as if being smothered by the air that now came across it.

No one spoke. Terror had stolen their words. The tribesman holding the babbling man held a hand over his mouth in an effort to quiet him. Everyone could sense the danger that now surrounded them.

Several rifles were now aimed outwards into the blackness. Their eyes were telling them that there was nothing out there, but their other senses knew better. They could sense a presence in the darkness. Something that was more malevolent than anything they had ever encountered.

A sound drifted across the empty plains to their ears. It was nothing they had heard before, not the grunting of a camel nor the call of one of the many foxes which wandered the desert. Instead, it resembled a whisper. A light, furtive, fluttering that seemed to barely kiss their ears.

Every man in the camp shivered. And it had nothing to do with the chill of the night air, for the raging fire still kept that at bay. This chill was a deeper one than the mere sense of touch. A feeling that bubbled up from deep within their lizard brains.

The leader of the group had had enough. He ordered that their camp be packed and that the camels be brought. Three men stood guard while the rest packed up camp. One more still held the shivering, bony form of the babbling man.

The Bedouin packed up at a speed seldom seen. It took them less than five minutes before they were ready to leave. Their camels were so terrified of whatever was out in the night that they foamed at the mouth and refused to let their masters ride them. The only choice left to everyone was to walk, which they did.

They chose a direction that they knew led to the nearest settlement. A place where they could find shelter from whatever evils had been brought upon them by this strange figure. The camels almost refused to be led, doing their best to hold position around the relative safety of the fire. But they were soon persuaded to move.

The group got on their way, keeping up as brisk a pace as they dared, unwilling to go too fast for risk of injury or snake bite. The odd whispering followed them for what seemed like hours. That bizarre fluttering would come in close, then melt away into the blackness once more.

At one point, one of the men let off a shot. The deafening crack of the rifle made everyone jump and the stranger started to babble incoherently once more. It took some doing to calm him.

There was not a word spoken as they walked. And for anyone who knows the Bedouin and their ways, this was most unusual. But no one had the heart or the inclination to chat. They just wanted to get to safety as soon as possible.

When they finally arrived at the settlement, it was noon the next day. The entire party was exhausted, their feet dry and cracked, their lips bleeding. Their state of fatigue was so great that they simply collapsed near the village well, relieved to be safe.

Once the party were fed and settled, the people of the village asked what had happened. Not one man would say, instead opting to remain silent in the face of the question. If pressed, they would just say that they were only alive by the grace of Allah.

Yet the crazy man continued to babble. Most of it was nonsense, some not even in Arabic, but some made sense.

Something was hiding in the desert, in an ancient city thought destroyed by the will of God Himself. He had seen great riches, matched only by the danger that dwelled out in the emptiness of the sands.

"Doom," he said through cracked, broken lips, "doom is coming!"

CHAPTER 2

Muscat, Sultanate of Muscat and Oman, 1933

Doctor Richard Race's shoes clacked noisily on the concrete floor of the *Al Rahma Hospital* as he walked uncertainly down its halls. He hadn't a clue where he was going since his escort, British Political Agent Colonel Stanley, had told him to head down the corridor and stop when he heard the screaming.

Not for the first time that day did Race wonder why His Majesty's Government had deemed it necessary that he should be contacted for this assignment. From what he'd been told of the man that had walked into the Bedouin camp a few nights prior, he was quite mad. Why the ravings of a mad man would be of any importance whatsoever, Race did not know.

Yet here he was, peering uncertainly into each room he passed, hoping to find that very lunatic. All he'd seen so far were the usual hospital affair of white linen pulled neatly across threadbare mattresses that sat on white metal frames. There was not a nurse in sight, much to Race's confusion. One would have thought them as essential to hospitals as doctors.

Then again, the ward itself did seem to be particularly devoid of life. Not a single room had patients in it, giving Race the feeling that he was quite alone in that stuffy white corridor. He shivered. He'd never liked hospitals at the best of times, but the eerie atmosphere of this one was utterly unnerving.

"I see you've not found him yet, doctor," came a voice from behind him.

Much to his shame, Race almost leapt out of his immaculately polished shoes. He looked around at the man who had spoken, clutching at his heart.

"Dammit man!" Race exclaimed. "You tell me there is a lunatic about the place and then proceed to sneak up behind me!"

Colonel Stanley, who looked very much like many other Colonels of his age in the British Army, chortled. His impressive bushy white moustache bristled oddly as he did so, looking to Race like a living thing on the man's top lip.

"I'm sorry, old man," Stanley said, "but I thought that since the ward was clear, it would be easy to find the chap."

"You mean to say that they cleared out an entire ward just for this one man?"

Stanley nodded. "The nurses will not go near him. And the other patients got to complaining of his ravings at night."

"Sweet Lord," Race breathed. "He seems quiet now."

"Yes indeed. Though that is strange. He is in the room at the end of the corridor. Come along, now. We must hurry."

"Colonel, may I ask again why I have been summoned here? I must get back to the British Museum in London as soon as possible. There is important work that needs to be done."

"Trust me, old man, this is much more interesting. But you must hear it for yourself."

Race followed Stanley as the man strode down the corridor. Even with a companion, the ward seemed to drip with malice. It was as if the rays of the brilliant sunshine outside would not dare peek through the windows into this dark place.

They stopped at the last room. The Colonel stepped aside, motioning Race forward. He saw the patient at once, tied to a bed near the window. He was deathly pale, with skin stretched so thin over his bones that the lines of his skeleton could be seen quite clearly. His hair and beard were black, wiry, and unkempt, sticking out from the man's head in odd directions.

But it was the eyes that held Race's attention.

Dark, staring orbs that had barely any white in them at all. They rolled around in the man's skull like a chameleon's, darting about the place in rapid succession. As Race walked closer, the eyes rolled towards him, fixing him with a gaze that stopped him in his tracks.

A burble of Arabic emerged from the man's lips, only barely audible. Race, who spoke several languages fluently, only just caught the words. He shivered and inched closer to the man on the bed.

The patient strained at his restraints, what was left of his muscle going taught with the effort. The eyes began to roll again, up and down, left and right, diagonally even. It looked like they weren't even attached to the optic nerve in the man's head anymore. Yet, somehow, he could still see.

"Do they know what's wrong with him?" Race whispered.

"The doctors are flummoxed, I'm afraid. They say it's like he's been starved and kept from drinking for months. That's the only reason that his tissues could have degraded so much. But food and water seem to do nothing for him. If his condition does not improve soon, he doesn't have much longer."

Race pulled up a chair to sit next to the dying patient. He hesitated a moment before taking the fellow's hand in his. It was as light as a feather, but its grip was tight as steel.

"My dear man," Race said soothingly, "I am so sorry this has happened."

The man's eyes stopped rolling around and focused on Race once more. For a moment, his constant twitching calmed. Then his lips started to move.

At first there was no sound, until slowly, words started to find their way past those cracked lips. Race had to lean in close to catch what was being said, and even then had trouble, because the man kept switching languages mid-sentence. Some words would be in Arabic, some in English, others in Portuguese, and yet more in a language entirely alien to Race's well-trained ear.

But what remained consistent throughout was the incredulity of it all.

The man spoke of nightmare creatures that stole men's souls. Of rooms piled high with glittering gold artefacts and coins. And of other terrors too awful to repeat in any language.

"My God," Race breathed, after having listened to the man talk for five minutes.

"What is it?" Stanley asked.

"Get me a pen and paper, man! I must write this down. He is speaking of The Atlantis of the Sands!"

CHAPTER 3

Darkness had crept over the Sultanate of Muscat and Oman without Race realising. He hadn't even heard the evening call to prayer, so engrossed was he in his writing of the unfortunate patient's ramblings.

He looked at his watch. It was well into the early morning. He had pages and pages of notes written down in his almost illegible shorthand. As he'd been fond of telling his teachers at Oxford, all that mattered was that *he* could read it.

The man had finally stopped talking and fallen into a deep slumber. Not that that affected his body in any meaningful way, as it continued to twitch and spasm intermittently. Race couldn't shake the feeling that he was watching a man get eaten from the inside out by some malevolent force beyond his understanding.

He suppressed a shudder at the horrible thought. The room suddenly felt a few degrees colder, as if thinking of the fellow's condition had sucked what little warmth there was out of the air. Race wrapped his arms about himself, wishing that he'd brought his coat.

The hospital was deathly silent. The only sound was the laboured breathing of the man in the restraints. It was not entirely unusual. The building itself had only been built some two decades earlier. Not everyone in the city had the funds to pay for medical care.

Even though Race knew he was being paranoid, he stood and walked to the window. It looked out onto the main street that ran in front of the hospital. It was where ambulances were supposed to bring emergency cases to be treated.

The street itself was empty. Completely devoid of any form of life. Race watched it for a few minutes, trying to quell the creeping sense of dread that had begun to curl its icy fingers around his guts.

He turned and walked out of the room into the hall beyond. The lights were on, so at least the electricity was still working. He did not relish exploring a hospital in the pitch darkness.

Race was about to call out for a nurse when he remembered what Stanley had told him earlier. The entire floor had been cleared. He'd have to head downstairs to find someone to talk to.

Thinking of Stanley made Race begin to wonder where he had disappeared to. He had no memory of the old Colonel telling him that he was leaving. Not surprising, considering how deeply engrossed in his writing he'd been, but it was still worrying. The old military man had been a comforting presence. Solid, commanding. Now it was sorely missed.

Race looked over at the man in the bed. He seemed alright. His ravings had obviously taken their toll on the poor man, leading Race to believe that this was the best sleep the fellow had gotten in ages. Surely, it would be alright to leave him for a minute or two?

The doctor was wracked with indecision. Perhaps Stanley had just popped downstairs for a moment to get some tea? Race hoped that was the case, because he did not want to be alone at that moment. His senses were telling him that there was danger in the hospital. Although he knew that that was ridiculous.

He was in a civilised country, in a nice, clean hospital staffed entirely by sane, sensible people. He was in as much danger as he would be in his rooms at Oxford. But he could not shake the feeling that something was wrong. Even in the harsh, bright lights of the electric bulbs, he felt that danger was creeping up on him from out of the darkness.

Race tucked his notebook into his jacket pocket, and his mind made up, started down the corridor towards the stairs that led down to reception. He was being silly, he realised. Daft, even. There was no danger. The mad man's proclamations of doom and nightmarish creatures had simply put him on edge. That was all.

As he walked, his footsteps echoed hollowly off the walls of the empty hallway. He tried to lighten his step, but it seemed to make no difference. Each time he put his foot down it was as if a bomb had gone off. It bounced off the walls, leading him to feel that it could be heard for miles around.

Race's heart was thumping now. His gut was telling him that all was not well. And some part of his subconscious, a small part that had survived thousands of years of evolution and danger, was telling him to get out of that place as soon as he could.

He continued onward, past the many empty rooms, getting closer and closer to the stairs. He was only a few feet away when a figure stepped into view.

It was that of a man, judging by the size. He was clad entirely in black robes. Even his face was wrapped, leaving only his eyes visible. In one hand he carried a revolver, and in the other, a vicious looking dagger made of a metal that was blacker than petroleum. It shimmered oddly in the light, looking like it was dancing in the man's hand.

If there was a situation in which a man with a revolver and a knife meant one no harm, Race could not think of it. The man's eyes bore an eerie similarity to the man in the hospital bed. They were almost entirely black, like two onyx orbs were set in his skull in place of eyes. And they were focused on Race.

Doctor Race hadn't always been an archaeologist. Like many men his age, he had served in the Great War. In those horrific, muddy, rat-infested trenches, he had learned that life was not all opulent rooms and fine teas. Sometimes it was based on snap decisions that meant the difference between living and dying.

It was time to make such a decision.

Race dove sideways before the man in black could react, heading straight for the open doorway to his right. The revolver fired just as Race crossed the threshold, landing hard on his side.

He scrambled to his feet immediately, desperately casting about for a weapon. In the hall, he could hear the steady, deliberate footsteps of his foe coming closer. The doctor grabbed the first thing he could get his hands on and pressed himself up against the wall to wait.

Race did his best to steady his breathing, which was threatening to give away his position. He thought back to what he had learned in the trenches and slowed his thudding heart. Outside, the footsteps stopped.

Time itself seemed to slow to a painful crawl. The hospital was still silent, even though the gunshot should by rights have aroused some suspicion. Race could hear no sound from the man that he knew was just outside the room.

Come on, you bastard! Race thought.

At last, a single footstep broke the deathly silence. Then another. And finally, the man in the black robes appeared through the doorway, his weapon held out in front of him. Race swung the thing he held in his hand, one of the polished metal stands that held the IV bottles.

It connected with the stranger's outstretched arm. The revolver went off in a brilliant explosion of sound, heat, and light. Its proximity to Race's head meant that he was almost knocked senseless by it. But the doctor's blow had the desired effect.

The revolver came out of the man's hand and Race pushed his advantage. He let go of his makeshift weapon, grabbed the man by the wrist, and yanked him forward with such force that the fellow came tumbling into the room in a flurry of black cloth.

As the figure came forward, Race brought his elbow down on the back of the chap's neck, putting all his weight behind the blow. The figure hit the floor hard, the strange dagger flying from his grasp and clattering to the floor. Race wasted no time lunging for the revolver, snatching it up off the floor and aiming it at the crumpled form.

"Right," he said, "I think you'll find I've got the upper hand, old chap. Tell me who the devil you are!"

A bizarre, unearthly fluttering noise at the window distracted the doctor for a split second. But it was all the time that the man on the floor needed.

Before he knew what was happening, Race felt himself grabbed by the lapels of his suit and tossed clean across the room. He hit the wall with an almighty crash, his head impacting the brickwork less than a second later, sending him falling into unconsciousness.

CHAPTER 4

Race awoke to the sight of Stanley's brilliant moustache hovering over him. He groaned, leading Colonel Stanley to let out a sigh of relief. In seconds, a nurse was by Race's side, busily checking him over.

"We thought we'd lost you, old chap," Stanley said.

"Where am I?" Race asked.

"Still in the hospital. We found you in a heap in one of the empty rooms. Looks like there was some kind of fight."

Race massaged his head and nodded. "There was. A man in black. I got distracted and the blighter got the better of me. I was sure he'd kill me."

"Ah. They weren't here for you, I'm afraid."

"The patient from the desert?"

"Indeed. What your assailant did to him... let's just say it wasn't pleasant."

Race noticed the nurse blanch at the mention of the incident. He suppressed a shiver, glad that the light of day was streaming in through the window.

"You'll be fine, Mister Race," the nurse, who was American, said. "Just a bump on the head. No concussion. I'll leave you and the Colonel to it."

"Any idea who this fellow was that attacked you?" Stanley asked once the nurse had left.

"No clue, I'm afraid. He was dressed in black robes, carried a Webley revolver and some kind of strange dagger."

"We found the revolver. Part of a shipment of British Army weapons that went missing a year or so ago. No dagger though. Arab, do you think?"

"Impossible to tell. He did not speak. In fact, he barely made a sound, even when I coshed him on the back of the head. Strong as a bloody ox, I'll say that much."

Stanley thought for a moment. "I'll get word to my sources. Perhaps they can give us something to go on. Did you get anything from the mad man?"

Race sat up suddenly and grasped at his pocket. He let out a relieved sigh upon realising that his notebook was still there.

"Indeed," he said, patting his breast. "Although, I will have to take a couple of days to decipher it. So much of what the man said was gibberish."

"But you're sure he spoke of the Atlantis of the Sands?"

Race nodded. "The fabled lost city of Ubar, yes."

"And riches too?" Stanley's eyes glittered at the mention of gold.

"Indeed, colonel. If what that man said is true, then we are looking at the greatest archaeological find since Carter found Tutankhamun."

"My God," Stanley breathed. "I can only imagine the joy of such a find."

"*If* it turns out to be true, my dear man. The poor fellow was quite out of his mind, after all."

"But why the need to murder a madman if his rantings were pure fiction?"

"A lot of what humanity does to itself is mad, as I'm sure you'll know."

Stanley nodded sombrely, thinking of his time in war. The things that he had seen men do to one another beggared belief. Yet, the thought of such a great find, of such riches, sparked the old soldier's imagination in ways that had not happened since he'd read of the great Quartermain's exploits as a much younger man.

"I want you to find out, doctor," Stanley said. "And quickly. I must make a report to His Majesty as soon as possible. If we can find this lost city, it will be a great feather in our caps. A knighthood could very well be in our future, my dear fellow."

Race swung his legs over the edge of the bed, pausing just long enough for the little gnomes in his head to stop tap-dancing, before he stood.

"Very well, colonel," he said. "But first, I need a drink, a coffee, and breakfast. Then I can begin trawling through my notes in search of the truth of the poor man's words. Will he be buried, do you think?"

Stanley waved his hand. "The hospital will take care of that."

Race thought for a moment. "A pauper's funeral, then?"

"I expect so."

"Find out for me, will you? And if that is indeed the case, tell the hospital that I will pay for the proper administration of whatever funeral rites they deem fit. I assume he was a native of this place, so he should be treated as such."

"If you're sure, doctor. Although I can't for the life of me think why it should matter. You did not know the man!"

"Respect for our fellow man, be they alive or dead, is one of the few things that separate us from the animals, colonel. It'll do well for you to remember that."

CHAPTER 5

Race had the good fortune to have been put up in one of Muscat's finest hotels by His Majesty's Government. Situated near the bazaar in the centre of the city, not far off from the Sultan's palace, it was a square building made of brilliant white stone, like so many others in the city.

Presently, Race was lounging in his chair smoking a Turkish cigarette, staring absentmindedly out of the window at the setting sun. Books of all sizes and languages were stacked about the place, along with several balled-up pieces of paper. He had stuck a map of The Empty Quarter on the wall above his desk, which had several pins in it. On the desk itself sat the notebook from the previous night and several empty inkwells.

The sun bathed the city in an eerie red glow that took one's breath away, no matter how many times it was seen. From his room, Race could see way out into the harbour, where ships and boats of all shapes and sizes were pulling in from a day's work. An English battleship sat just off the coast, looking out of place among the native vessels.

The transcribing had turned out to be a more tedious process than Race had anticipated. Not only was he translating various languages, but he also found that his Portuguese was somewhat lacking. He was also struggling over whether or not to include the man's multiple prophecies of doom or his descriptions of terrible creatures too big to be real.

His scientific mind was telling him to include it all. But there was just so much of it. It appeared that the man had been seeing perfectly ordinary desert creatures as nightmarish entities bent on his destruction. Although, if the man in black had been anything to go by, then perhaps he had been right to be afraid.

Race's thoughts once again drifted to that man, trying in vain to remember anything that might help him identify the fellow. But all he could think of was those eyes. Eyes that no normal human being could ever possess. And the sheer strength of the chap disturbed him, as well.

He cast a glance at his map once more. His lack of knowledge of the famous *Rub' al Khali* was making his job harder. He'd never had the opportunity nor the inclination to trek through that vast expanse of arid sand. What he needed, Race decided, was an expert.

A knock on the door pulled him out of his musings. Race opened it to discover the smiling face of Colonel Stanley, dressed not in khaki military fatigues, but for dinner.

"Thought you could use a bite to eat, old chap," Stanley said. "And I've had an idea."

At the mention of food, Race's stomach informed him that it was well and truly empty. So he told the Colonel to meet him downstairs after he had dressed for dinner.

"What we need," Stanley said once Race had met up with him, "is an explorer. Someone who knows the desert like the back of their hand."

"I was thinking just that in my room. I need help pinpointing exactly where the city might be located. Some local knowledge would be invaluable."

Dinner was an hour away when the two of them arrived at the restaurant. The waiter assured them that they had a table and showed them to the bar to wait. The only other person there – besides the bartender – was a skinny man in a fedora that was hunched over a notebook. His creased, khaki linen suit hung loose on his scrawny frame, and he appeared for all the world like a scarecrow that had decided to leave the fields and grab himself a drink.

He looked up from his frantic scribblings as Race and Stanley took their seats, still discussing who would be the best candidate to act as a guide. Race noticed that he was a handsome man, with fine cheekbones and a strong jaw. A pencil moustache adorned his upper lip and his pale grey eyes watched them curiously as they spoke.

"It's quite rude to stare, old boy," Stanley said upon noticing those intelligent eyes upon him.

"I'm sorry," he said, his accent distinctly American, "but I couldn't help but overhear that you need a guide for a desert trek. I might be able to help you out."

"You don't look like an explorer," Stanley said.

The man chuckled. "I'm not. But I know of a bird that is."

He produced an American newspaper from somewhere within the pockets of his jacket with a flourish, slapping it on the bar with the front-page headline visible. The man slid it across the marble bar towards the two Englishmen and tapped knowingly on the headline print.

Van Alden Crosses Empty Quarter! First American to Accomplish Such a Feat!

"And said explorer happens to be in this very hotel," the stranger said.

"How do you know this Van Alden?" Race asked, skimming over the print below the headline.

"I wrote the story. My name is Jimmy Alsop."

He extended a bony hand. Race noticed that the man had absurdly long fingers. They seemed to stretch further than any other he had ever seen. Introductions were made in short order, although Stanley himself seemed less than impressed by the man's credentials and suggestions.

"Why should we put our trust in a reporter from America?" Stanley asked.

Alsop shrugged. "Just trying to help, is all."

"I've never met a Yank who isn't trying to help himself more than anyone else."

Alsop smiled as he pulled out a cigarette. He lit it carefully, inhaled, and took a moment to savour the tobacco as it filled his lungs before he spoke again. Race noticed that Stanley took the delay badly, the set of his jaw showing how angry he was.

"Look, I ain't trying to chisel nothing out of you. Just that I got this nose for a story, see, and I can't help but notice that you two birds seem to be talking about a big one."

"Just like an American to stick his nose where it doesn't belong," Stanley said.

Race had finished reading the story in the newspaper. He folded it neatly before placing it on the table and sliding it back to Alsop. He looked at the American then, studying his eyes. The sardonic smile remained fixed on the fellow's face under the scrutiny.

"Apart from your obvious mistakes in spelling, that's quite a yarn you've spun about this Van Alden," Race said at last.

"It's no yarn. I don't make my dough by lying to the public. I'd have to be some kind of twit."

Stanley snorted. Race ignored him.

"If Van Alden is half as good as you say, then I think we've found the perfect companion for this adventure."

Stanley started to protest. The Colonel had spent enough time around Americans and American diplomats in the last few years to form strong opinions about the lot of them. Opinions which were not to be voiced in polite company by a gentleman.

"Van Alden is all that and more besides. And I can make the introductions. All you gotta do is promise to give me the scoop."

Race held out his hand once more.

"It's a deal."

CHAPTER 6

The heavy knocking on her room door roused Jacqueline "Jaq" Van Alden from her restless slumber. She came awake with a start and a curse, her mind questioning just where in the hell she was, as was common with sudden awakening from afternoon naps.

Her fingers found the blasted switch at last and light, brilliant and hurtful to the eyes, flooded the tiny room. The damnable banging on the door continued, forcing her to shout that she was indeed coming.

"Keep your damn hat on!" She called.

Jaq swung her legs off the bed to the floor, seriously considering just going back to sleep. After, of course, telling the annoying pest outside the room to go to the bowels of hell from whence they came. A glance at the clock told her that it was time for dinner, however, so she stood and made her way over to the door.

It swung open to reveal Jimmy Alsop, the gangly news reporter that had just interviewed her a few days before, although she had known him for far longer than that. Long enough for her to snarl upon seeing his handsome, smiling features looming over her.

"Is that any way to greet an old friend?" Alsop said, his damnable smile still firmly in place.

Jaq turned her back on him, heading into her room and snatching the bottle of bourbon from her bedside table. She took a good glug of the throat-burning stuff before answering.

"I don't know where you get the idea that we're friends, Jimmy," she spat. "What is it you want, greaseball?"

"Well, ain't you just as cute as a bug's ear tonight, Jaq," Jimmy said. "I come bearing gifts, as a matter of fact."

"You ain't ever given a lady anything she wanted before, Jimmy. So, you'll excuse me if I'm wary."

"Since you ain't no lady, Jaq, I'll not be ruining my reputation by telling you that there are two respectable gentleman downstairs looking for a desert guide."

Jaq paused in her rummaging of her suitcase for something to wear to dinner. She gave Alsop a look that was part curiosity, part surprise, and a very large part wariness.

"What do you get out of the deal? Dough?"

"You think so little of me. I get a good scoop, and the chance to come with you."

Jaq snorted. "Why would they bring your scrawny ass along?"

"Because, in return for me introducing you, you're going to tell them that I will be an invaluable companion."

This time, Jaq almost bent double as the laugh came out of her. The very idea of Alsop coming along on any type of desert adventure was absurd, let alone him asking her to suggest him. Yet that cunning, sardonic smile didn't budge from the face of the reporter, as he leaned against the doorframe and watched her laugh.

"You're serious, aren't you?"

Alsop nodded. "Without me, the introductions won't be made. Without me singing your praises, they won't hire you. Without you getting this sweet job, well," he held out his hands, "I doubt there are many in this town willing to hire dames. And you need the money, Jaq."

"Damn you, Jimmy," Jaq snarled.

It was true, she did need the money. Her last expedition had been a great one for knowledge, but it had drained her purse. And Alsop was right, there weren't many who were willing to hire women to explore the desert.

As Jaq had found out after it became her great passion, being an explorer required money. Lots of it. Since she had come from humble Texan ranch hands, that was something she didn't have much of. Not to mention that she was frequently passed over for grants in favour of her male counterparts by the eminent universities of the world.

"You're a damned greaseball, Jimmy," she said, "and when you die, you're going straight to the fiery gates of hell."

"Is that a yes?"

She gave a reluctant nod. "Make the introductions and you get to come. Although I don't know how I'll swing it."

That damn smile again. "I'll give you such a good profile that they'll hang off your every word. Meet me downstairs in the dining hall. I'll be with the gentlemen in question. And dress up nice, why don't you?"

Jaq slammed the door after the infernal reporter, and considered, not for the first time, if shooting the little jerk was worth the hassle. She concluded that it wasn't. Not yet, anyway, so she got herself dressed for dinner, making sure to take swigs of bourbon in-between to make the process more agreeable.

***

So it was that Jacqueline Van Alden, the tall, lean, handsome woman with green eyes and short, wavy raven hair came to join Doctor Race and Colonel Stanley for dinner. Except that since she had not deemed a dress necessary for a trek across the desert, she wore khaki pants and a white linen shirt.

While the staff of the hotel were much too polite to comment on such indecency, a few of the guests were less inclined. She suppressed a smirk at the muttering of the older English gentlemen and ladies who had dressed appropriately for dinner.

Jaq spotted her table immediately, since even sitting down, Alsop was just that much taller than everyone else. She immediately guessed that Stanley was a military man of some description, and would have pinned him as English by his reaction to her confident stride alone.

The other man was much more interesting. He didn't react upon seeing her as she had come to expect, which was a shame. It was only in the wilder parts of the world that she was allowed to indulge her little habit of throwing dining rooms into disarray with her appearance. At home she was always proper, unless one tried to speak to her. Her Texan drawl and tendency to swear were impossible to hide in even the politest company.

Yet the men at the table, discounting Alsop of course, did what gentlemen do when a lady pulls out a chair to join them. They stood and greeted her warmly. Although the bird with the moustache still had a look of complete surprise on his face.

"Jaqueline Van Alden, I assume?" Race said.

Jaq smelt the distinct aroma of the Turkish cigarettes the man was smoking. She couldn't resist asking for one. Once it had been given and lit, she replied to his question.

"Call me Jaq. Everyone does. My friend Jimmy tells me you two need a guide?"

"Perhaps," Race said after introductions had been made, "but right now I think that we should get to know one another. Business talk and a fine meal do not mix very agreeably in one's stomach, I find."

And so the evening commenced, with Alsop playing his usual role of grifter. The man had a way with words second only to the greatest writers of the age. It was one of his very few finer qualities, and it came in handy on this occasion to help convince Race and Stanley of her merits as an explorer.

Not that she wasn't a great explorer. She had trekked through the Empty Quarter, made friends with Bedouins, met great Sultans, and negotiated treaties that would go a long way to keeping peace within the region. Not to mention what she had done in the vast, untamed wilds of her own home country.

But as Alsop had so succinctly put it, many a man tended not to put too much stock into the words of a woman.

"Not since Gertrude Bell has such an explorer existed!" Alsop said, finishing a story that had taken him almost five minutes to recount.

Jaq had been watching the two Englishmen while Alsop said his piece, and by the looks on their faces, the reporter might as well have been telling fairy stories. She stubbed her cigarette out in the ashtray, hard enough to get their attention, then leaned forward in her seat.

"Let's cut the bullshit, shall we?" she said. "I know the desert like the back of my hand. You two need someone like me to take you somewhere inside the *Rub' al Khali*, and right now gentlemen, there is no one better within easy reach. I know the area, the natives, and how to survive. You may or may not have trouble with me being a woman. I don't really give a damn. Cause in the end, the choice is up to you, partner. But I give you my word that if you choose me, we will get where you need to go. That's for sure and for certain."

Race smiled. Stanley looked put off by the language used. Alsop still resembled a greaseball. Silence reigned.

"If what you have just said is true," Race said, "then there is just one more thing to ask you, Miss Van Alden."

"And what is that?"

"How are you with mortal danger?"

CHAPTER 7

Colonel Stanley was understandably unhappy when he awoke the next morning. Unfortunately for Race, he also happened to be an early riser. So, it was at the crack of dawn, as the morning call to prayer drifted lazily over the misty draped buildings of Muscat, that the good Colonel was at his door.

"Is it because she's a woman?" Race asked, rubbing his sleep-filled eyes.

"No. It is because they are *Americans*! Blasted Yanks! You never can trust them, mark my words. It took them a bloody age to get involved in the war, and if there ever is another, they will do the same until it suits them!"

Race sighed heavily. Stanley was much too animated for such an early hour. Race would have preferred a couple hours more sleep and a cup of coffee – or three – before discussing business like this.

"Calm down, man," Race said. "If you can find us another guide by the end of the day, then by all means, go ahead. But you and I both know that there is no one in this city who would be able to do it at such short notice. There are dark forces at work, Colonel, and I'd rather they not beat us to the find of the century!"

Stanley stopped his incessant pacing to give Race a pained look. It was the look of a man who knew he was beat, but that didn't mean he had to like it.

"Look, colonel," Race said, "we need their help. If that newspaper article is even half true then this Van Alden woman is a damn good explorer. When it comes down to it, this is *our* expedition, on behalf of the British Government. Funding will come from His Majesty, not the President. What we need to worry about now is not anything to do with the Americans. I need you to get to the consulate and start the process of getting the money."

"You're right, of course. But you need to keep your eyes on those two. Especially that damned Alsop fellow. The chap is a bad egg."

"Understood. Go get some breakfast, old man. I'll dine with Van Alden and Alsop and see if we can find a route to this fabled city."

Stanley nodded before leaving, at last, giving Race a chance to get dressed. No matter what part of the world he found himself in, Race always liked to dress well when he could. The heat of Oman necessitated linen suits, so he chose a simple dark green three piece affair, with a matching hat.

Jaq was already downstairs with a cup of coffee and a newspaper. Her plate sat empty in front of her, the remains of bacon and eggs only just visible on it. Race asked if he could join her before ordering eggs and a full pot of black coffee.

"Thought you limeys only went in for tea?" She asked.

Race shook his head. "Coffee keeps me awake better than any cup of tea. Besides, there is nothing quite like the coffee in this part of the world. It came from around these parts, did you know? They used to call it the "wine of Araby"."

"It certainly is better here than it ever was in the States. A cup from an American diner will put hairs on your chest, that's for sure and for certain. But it tastes like sludge."

"Not had the pleasure, I'm afraid. So, have you thought about our offer last night?"

Jaq nodded. "Of course, there'll need to be contracts drawn up and all. Once that's done, it would be a pleasure to accompany you on your fool's errand."

"You do not believe it exists then?"

"I ain't saying I been everywhere in that big expanse of desert, but I've been across a fair chunk of it. I've talked to people who live out there. That die out there. They spend their time criss-crossing that expanse of nothing like we walk down city streets. And not once have I heard tell of this Atlantis of the Sands being real."

"So why agree to guide us?"

Jaq sighed. "Because it's what I do, Doctor Race. I could lie to you and say all kinds of things, but the fact is that I like it out there. A person sees things differently out there. Experiences things that most just don't do in this civilised world of ours. An' I'll take a couple of mad Englishmen on their search for *El Dorado* if I get paid for it."

"There was a time when people believed all kinds of things about the world that we know now are untrue. Nobody believed that Carter would find Tutankhamun! Or how about how the great Incan city of Machu Picchu went undiscovered for hundreds of years despite its size!"

"I like that you get excited over your work, doctor. But until I lay my eyes on this city of yours, I don't think I'll ever fully believe."

"Perhaps I will change your mind, Miss Van Alden."

"Care to wager on that?" Alsop said.

He had appeared quite suddenly, sliding out a chair and sitting down before either Race or Jaq had seen him approach. The fedora still adorned his head and a cigarette hung loose from the corner of his mouth, as if he had forgotten it was there.

"Come on," he said, "what's life without a bit of risk? I imagine Doctor Race has deep pockets. And you were just telling me last night how you could use the dough, weren't ya Jaq?"

The look she gave Alsop would have melted a man with more scruples into a slurry. Alsop, however, just smiled that smile of his and kept eye contact.

"I'm not really a betting man, Mister Alsop," Race said. "I've seen too many a man lose entirely too much money on foolish bets."

"Come on, doc, this ain't no fool's bet, is it? If you's so confident the city is real, then why not put your money where your mouth is?"

"If the lady is agreeable, then perhaps."

Jaq only just managed to stop herself from glaring at Alsop. The man was making it hard to keep up the charade of friendship. She considered her options. Eventually, she leaned forward and extended her hand.

"A wager it is."

***

Jaq had been studying the map pinned to Race's room wall for five minutes. She kept referencing his notes and tracing her finger over various parts of the map as she did so. Race watched her work, keenly interested in her map reading skills. He was no navigator, even occasionally getting lost within his home city of London.

Alsop was casually leaning against the windowsill, smoking cigarette in one hand and gin and tonic in the other. Smoke drifted lazily about the room, stirred by the slight breeze coming in through the open window. Race found himself growing an intense dislike for the man's brand of cigarettes.

"So, what's the scoop on this Ubar place, then?" Alsop asked. "You're acting like it's the find of the century, doc, and yet Jaq over here don't even believe in the place."

"You want to take this, doctor?" Jaq said.

Race smiled, the gleeful feeling of boyish wonder that he often felt when discussing ancient history bubbling up within him. He leaned forward in excitement to tell the tale that he had been so intrigued by for so many years.

"Ubar is a city that shouldn't exist! You see that great expanse of desert on that map that represents The Empty

Quarter? Nothing can thrive there, let alone a great city. And yet, the Atlantis of the Sands did just that! Ancient Assyrian texts say that it was a city of great wealth. The centre of one of the expensive trades to ever dominate this region in the ancient world – the spice trade. It is said that they grew so wealthy that all its people lived like kings!

But in doing so, they rejected the word of God Himself. Islamic texts say that they were a perverted, pagan people, whose only goal was pleasure. Stories of the place have drifted from one person to another for centuries, especially among the Bedouin people. That the people of Ubar were given more than one chance to turn towards God and accept his word, but their wealth and hubris made them blind to His love. So, just as he had done with Sodom and Gomorrah, He destroyed them."

Alsop smirked. "We're looking for a city that God himself destroyed then? Sounds like these people knew how to have a good time."

"Of course, most scholars believe that these tales are nonsense. Utter poppycock. But if one studies the stories, one begins to see the truths in them. Most mention that God sent great winds to blow the city away. And the *Rub' al Khali* is known for its fierce winds. There are other titbits, of course, but trust me when I say that there is enough to believe that this city did indeed exist! And now with this man who wandered out of the desert–"

"This mad man," Jaq interjected.

"I'll grant you that, my dear lady. Yet if he was so mad and there was no truth to his words, why was he killed?! You didn't sit there while he spoke. You didn't hear the truth in his words. I believe that this city exists."

"Well, if this don't beat all," Alsop said with a smirk. "Ain't ever been a time when I've felt more like I was in one of them pulp magazines before."

"True or not, this man's trek was erratic, to say the least," Jaq said. "Which makes sense, considering he was almost out of his mind. It makes tracking his movements hard."

"That's one of the problems I've been having," Race said. "Sources are unclear as to where Ubar might be located, but it seems as if he managed to miss all the most likely places. All my notes on his ramblings are in that book. You're welcome to borrow it."

"Good, I need to show it to someone."

"Can you trust them?"

She nodded. "I trust him with my life. He's a local Arab. Good man for this kind of thing. He's acted as my guide for as long as I've lived in this neck of the woods."

"Remember what I told you both last night. Someone doesn't want the city revealed. We have to take care."

"If you trust me, you must take my word that this guy is a good egg. Ain't many men I'd trust with my life, but he is one of them."

CHAPTER 8

As Race and Jaq were descending the steps of the hotel towards the street, they found Colonel Stanley coming the other way. The fellow bore the look of a man who had spent a great many hours talking to the very stupid and the even more stubborn. Race had never seen Stanley look as if he could use a drink more.

"Where are you two off to?" He asked, pausing to mop the sweat from his brow.

"To an old friend of mine," Jaq said. "We need information."

"Jolly good. I just spent a few hours in the consulate convincing a bunch of fools of the importance of our mission. So, if you'll both excuse me, I could use a glass of very fine whiskey. I bid you both good day for now."

They watched him climb the steps and disappear inside the hotel.

"There's a man that has had quite a time of it," Race commented.

"I've met the staff at the consulate," Jaq said. "I'm surprised he's back so soon."

"I imagine the Colonel has a way of getting what he wants, regardless of who he asks. Military men like himself usually do. As for us, Miss Van Alden, I am putting myself entirely in your hands. Lead the way!"

And lead she did, refusing the offer of a ride from one of the many taxi men who waited outside the hotel. She later informed Race that walking was always best, no matter how great the distance, as it would help him get acclimatised to the heat before the expedition.

What a heat it was, too! Even though Race had been in the city for a few weeks by then, it was still staggering to think that any person could live in such conditions. The arid climate made one long for rain, and the almost complete lack of any vegetation projected the idea that nothing was supposed to live in such a place, let alone establish a society.

Yet the buildings that surrounded them, some white and some a kind of light brown, plus the abundance of robed men that walked the streets, showed that it was possible. The people themselves were the loud, chatty sort, and the harsh, barking tones of Arabic drifted to one's ears from every which way.

As they turned into the bazaar, the talking grew in intensity, as traders and shoppers haggled and bargained over wares. The place was lined with shops, selling everything from aromatic spices to brilliantly coloured materials. It was a far cry from the quiet, reserved atmosphere of even the busiest London store.

Race had to admit that it was a tad overwhelming. He'd never been the best amongst large crowds to begin with, but the sheer overload of sights, sounds, and smells, was enough to make him lightheaded.

Yet Jaq seemed to be in her element. She strode through the crowd as if it were her own family that she was amongst, fending off the advances of eager shop keepers with the practiced ease of a professional. All one had to do was watch her advance to know that this was not a woman who scared easily.

Which was why Race was so caught off-guard when she stopped suddenly and grabbed his arm. She leaned towards him, bringing her lips uncomfortably close to his ear.

"We're being watched," she breathed. "Follow my lead."

Race's heart picked up speed almost immediately, beating so hard within his chest that he feared it would alert whoever was watching them. Trying to be as discreet as he possibly could, he sought the crowd for danger, but its sheer density made it hard to distinguish one man from another, let alone pick out threats.

Jaq's hand slipped down his arm towards his, grasping it tightly. He let himself be led like that, hoping that to any observers it would look as if a keen young woman was showing her sweetheart something. He put an easy smile on his face to add to the impression.

On she led him through the great crowd of oblivious shoppers, his eyes doing their best to catch sight of their pursuers. It was the black that gave them away, for on a nearby rooftop he spotted it. A pitch-black head wrap bearing a remarkable similarity to the one worn by his assailant in the hospital.

"It is them," Race hissed, "the ones who attacked me the other night. On the roof!"

Jaq kept silent, but he saw her glance up towards the roofs above. She chose a side alley, seemingly at random, and suddenly they were leaving the market hubbub behind. The sounds of bartering started to fade as they rushed down the cramped space, until they emerged into the bright sunlight once more.

A glance behind them told Race that their pursuers were still after them. A man in black could be seen jogging down the alleyway in their direction. Jaq took Race across the street at a brisk pace and down another opening between two two-story buildings.

Race was keenly aware of the sound of footsteps as the man following picked up his pace. But so too did he and Jaq. They were running now, dodging down a littered side street barely big enough for a single motor vehicle. Two men sitting on a doorstep looked on at the strange sight of the two foreigners running past them in amusement, before going back to their smoking.

"Where are we going?" Race breathed.

The sweat flowed freely from his pores in the intense heat, causing the material of his suit to cling uncomfortably to his body as he ran. He was working hard to keep pace with the fit young woman, realising that it had been some time since he had been involved in any kind of physical activity.

"The man I mentioned," Jaq replied. "He'll protect us. Not far now."

The words were barely out of her mouth when they were forced to skid to a halt. At the end of the street, only a few feet away from them, two armed men had appeared. Both were dressed in the black robes that Race had come to recognise so well. He looked behind them to see the one who had been following them standing in the middle of the street.

They were trapped.

CHAPTER 9

For a moment, it seemed as if the outside world had vanished, leaving Race, Jaq, and the robed men as the only living creatures in existence. A deathly silence hung over the scene, broken only by the panting of Jaq and Race. No one spoke.

Three sets of eyes, each as dark as night, bore down upon the archaeologist and the explorer. The gazes kept the two rooted to the spot. Race could not shake the feeling that some dark form of witchcraft was working its devilish black magic upon them.

Then they heard it. The slow, methodical clacking of boots on concrete. It was faint at first, distant, but it approached steadily. It didn't take long for a fourth man, this one bigger than his three companions but similarly dressed, to step out of the shadows of a lonely alley to the left of the fellow behind them.

Race recognised the man's dagger almost immediately. He looked closer at the figure, trying to discern whether or not this was the same assailant from the hospital. The dagger shimmered gently, looking like waves in a dark pool were moving across it, even though there wasn't much light in the shadow of the buildings.

"Give us the book," said the big man.

His English was perfect and he had no immediately discernible accent, but Race knew that he had come from somewhere in the Middle East.

"What book?" Jaq asked.

"The book or death," the man replied.

In response, the other three men all raised their revolvers in unison. A dreadful chill ran through Race's blood as he stared down the barrel of the weapon. A chill he had not felt in a very long time.

"It's in my jacket pocket," Jaq said.

Race's mind was flicking through and discarding a thousand ideas of escape a minute. He didn't want to give up the book, but if it would save their lives, they had very little choice in the matter.

Jaq reached slowly in her jacket pocket to withdraw the leather-bound journal. The leader's eyes fixed on the thing almost immediately, giving Jaq and Race relief from his terrible gaze. Jaq threw the book forward with a weak underhand throw, such that it landed halfway between them and the leader.

"I never was very good at baseball," she said.

Race felt her hand grab his and knew immediately that she was planning something daring. She pulled his hand lightly to the left, causing him to turn his eyes in that direction. A small alcove could be seen there. He understood and gave Jaq's hand a squeeze to let her know.

But everything changed in an instant.

Just as the big man was advancing towards his prize, a rifle shot cracked off, echoing down the silent street. The man next to the leader fell suddenly, like a puppet with its strings cut, hitting the ground with a dull thump.

Jaq was moving already, dragging Race into the alcove just as the three remaining robed men opened fire with their revolvers. Another shot rang out, this one louder and closer than the first. Another man crumpled to the street.

Bullets impacted the wall next to Race's head, sending dust and bits of stone flying into the air. Jaq had pulled a pistol from within her jacket to return fire. The booming gunfire assaulted Race's ears with a ferocity that had once been so familiar. For his part, he kept himself pressed against the roughly carved wooden door of the alcove.

The leader was still in the picture, but he had hidden down the same alley he had come from. He was yelling something in Arabic to his one remaining follower, who was keeping Race and Jaq pinned down with revolver fire. The man was moving towards cover when a final rifle shot sounded and he too fell to the street.

Silence descended so suddenly that it surprised Race. His ears still rang, his heart still thumped, and the adrenaline still flowed like champagne at an affluent party.

"Do not go through with your plans!" Came the voice of the leader from somewhere unseen. "It will mean death for you and your friends. Mark my words, Doctor Race, this is not over!"

"Well, that was a riot," Jaq said, making sure the street was clear. "I wonder who saved our bacon?"

"Whoever they are, I am grateful," Race said.

He stepped tentatively out into the street, and when no bullets made their way through his chest, hurried over to scoop up the book.

"I cannot leave you alone for a moment, can I, *habib albi*?" Came a voice from above.

Both Jaq and Race looked up towards a rooftop two buildings away to see an Arab man waving at them. He asked them to wait, and in less than a minute, he was before them.

He was a skinny chap, with a long scraggly beard, heavily lined dark skin, and amber eyes, behind which Race sensed great kindness. The black hair on his head and beard was speckled with grey. His robes were simple, but immaculately clean. A beautifully kept Lee-Enfield Mark 1 rifle, used by the British Army before the Great War, was held across his chest.

"Abdulrahman!" Jaq exclaimed.

"Indeed," said the man with a warm smile, "I heard that a few foreigners had gotten in trouble in the streets of Muscat. I had to investigate. And thank *Allah* that I did."

"We are eternally grateful to you, good sir," Race said, extending his hand.

Introductions were made in short order.

"This is the man we were going to see, doc," Jaq said. "He has been my friend for many years."

Abdulrahman crouched by the body of one of the men. He removed the wrap around the head of the corpse to study the face.

"Do you know this man?" He asked.

Both Race and Jaq shook their heads. Abdulrahman repeated the process with the other bodies. They all seemed to be Arab men in remarkable shape. Well-fed and fit as oxen. Their weapons were well-kept, but apart from extra bullets, they carried nothing else that could identify them.

"Come my friends, we must leave before the army comes," Abdulrahman said. "We shall go to my house and you can tell me why four people you do not know are trying to kill you."

From the shadows, dark, white-less eyes watched them carefully, committing their faces to a memory that was older than it appeared. He felt nothing for these people, not hatred nor love, but a secret had to be protected, even if it meant their deaths.

CHAPTER 10

Race had often heard of the great aristocratic mansions of Oman, veritable oases located behind intricately carved Indian teak doors. Lavish places full of opulent furniture and expensive ornaments, their designs influenced by the whims and tastes of the rich mercantile class that ruled the country. Yet he had never had the pleasure of seeing one.

Until now.

Abdulrahman led them off the hot, dusty street, through a beautiful door bearing the geometric design of a fine Arab craftsman, and into a cool room that smelled of incense. The temperature difference was immediately noticeable, so much so that Race felt himself shiver suddenly in his sweat-soaked clothes.

"Welcome to my home," Abdulrahman said. "Come, we shall have some tea and talk."

He led Jaq and Race through several well-decorated rooms to an inner courtyard. A bubbling fountain sat in the centre of the square space, with several chairs arranged around it. The place radiated an air of peaceful mediation, putting the new visitors at ease almost immediately.

"Rich man," Race commented after they had been seated and their host hurried off to make tea.

"Maybe once," Jaq said, "but now, I think he'd tell you differently."

Race pondered that comment as Abdulrahman came back carrying a tray bearing an ornate silver teapot and three small cups. The tea was poured, the scent of it wafting to Race's nose, making him realise that almost every single cup of tea he had ever had in Oman was better than the ones in London.

"Why is it that you two were on your way to see me?" Abdulrahman asked. "The fact that Jaq is involved means that there is bound to be some kind of adventure that needs undertaking."

Race pulled the book from his pocket and handed it to their host. The man took it carefully, flipping through the pages to find out why it was so valuable. His eyes widened considerably as he skimmed the pages. A whistle escaped his lips.

"I assume those men were not willing to kill for a mere legend," he said at last. "You have found the lost city of Ubar?"

"Not yet," Jaq said. "Which is why we're here. We need your skills to help us."

"There are some secrets that are better left undiscovered," Abdulrahman said. "Ubar is one of them."

He closed the book gently before handing it back to a surprised Race.

"But sir! Think of what we could discover at such an ancient site!"

Abdulrahman smiled. "I am, Doctor Race. The desert has many legends. My people were a very nomadic race, until only recently. We did not keep many records, only those that passed from the mouth of one to another. Some tales still survive in bits and pieces. This one does."

"Isn't that reason enough to find it?"

"It does not survive because the tale is a good one. It is one of caution. Of warning. One that we must heed."

"It's too late now," Jaq said. "Those people want to kill us, and I highly doubt they'll stop just cause they failed one time. I got a feeling they gonna be coming for our hides a might harder now, and I'd rather die fighting than forgetting. That's for sure and for certain."

Abdulrahman laughed. "You will never change, will you *habib albi*?" He turned to Race. "When things become personal for her, then she's going to finish it, no matter what it is."

"They're not just personal for Miss Van Alden, sir," Race said. "Those brutes have attacked me twice now. The first time, they killed a man. A man who was so out of his mind he didn't know which way was up or down! That is unforgivable. I owe it to him to find this city. Legends be damned!"

The fire in Race's eyes shocked Jaq. Up to that point, he had been nothing but polite and mild mannered. A typical English gentleman, of the kind Jaq saw so often on her travels. Sometimes it was all show. An act to lure young ladies into their beds. But she had never seen such fire in one before.

"If we don't get your help," she said, "then we will be forced to find another guide. One more willing and much less capable."

"I am not worried for my health. It is you two that I worry for! I am an old man, with nothing left in the world but this house and some money. But you, Jaq, are young. Full of life. I do not wish to see you throw it away on a foolish quest for glory."

"All the more reason for you to agree to be our guide. Besides, it's too late for us to back out now. We're on someone's list. I doubt they'd give up if we just said we wasn't gonna go after the city."

Her friend sighed heavily and gently placed his empty teacup on the table.

"What I know of Ubar," he said gravely, "none of it is good. Greed was their downfall, but greed very easily breeds evil in men's hearts."

"We have both had experience with evil, sir," said Race. "We know how to handle it."

"I see that neither of you will be dissuaded from this venture. I have no choice but to help you, then, for I'm sure no one in this place cares for you as much as I do, Jaq."

"Thank you, my friend."

Abdulrahman took the book back, flipping through the pages once more. His brow furrowed in thought and he stood. He beckoned Jaq and Race to follow, leading them from the courtyard and its gurgling fountain back into the darkened rooms of his mansion.

They wound their way through lavish rooms towards the back of the residence, coming to a heavy door that had multiple locks on it. Abdulrahman withdrew a set of keys from within his robes and proceeded to unlock all of them before swinging the door open. He shuffled inside, his fingers finding the light switch beside the door.

"My word," Race exclaimed.

***

Back at the hotel, Colonel Stanley sucked thoughtfully on his ivory pipe as one of his soldiers relayed information about the shooting in town earlier. It was a worrying account, especially since there were reports that two white foreigners had been involved somehow, and now no one could find them.

"One of the incursions by the inner tribes?" Stanley suggested, referring to the raids that tribes from inner Oman sometimes carried out on the cities.

The man shrugged his shoulders. "No one is sure, sir."

"Keep looking for the two whites, alright? And keep me informed. Dismissed."

Alsop, who had been watching the exchange from one table over, ambled towards Stanley and pulled out a chair. He didn't so much sit as collapse into it, folding one long leg over the other fixing the Colonel with eyes that danced with interest.

"Sounds like our friends got into some trouble, chief," he said.

"Perhaps. I have my men out looking for Race and Miss Van Alden. We'll find them shortly, I'm sure."

"I'm sure."

"You don't seem that worried."

Alsop smiled.

"I know Miss Van Alden," he said, putting emphasis on the *'miss'*. "If you find bodies that aren't hers, then she's usually fine and dandy."

"Capable young woman, is she?"

"Indeed Colonel. Although I get the feeling that you don't like us much, do ya?"

Stanley puffed on his pipe, eying the reporter through the swirling smoke. "Whatever gave you that idea, old chap?"

"Call it journalistic instinct. Come on, Stanley, you can be honest. Drop the gentleman act for a while. I won't blame ya, chief."

"In my experience, most Yanks have never been too good in a crisis, old boy. But I'm always willing to let someone prove me wrong."

"I'm sure that Miss Van Alden and I will do just that."

"Good, because if you don't, I won't hesitate to put a bullet in your head, old boy," Stanley said coldly. "I won't have you endanger the lives of me or my men."

Alsop laughed and stood up. "I wouldn't worry about me, chief. I've done this before, see, and I *always* make it out alive."

Stanley watched the man leave as a feeling of deep unease washed over him. He wasn't worried about Miss Van Alden – he'd followed Gertrude Bell's career closely for years but there was something about Alsop that bothered him.

I'll be keeping my eye on you, my boy, Stanley thought bitterly as he emptied his pipe.

CHAPTER 11

The room that Abdulrahman had led them to was a treasure trove, not of gold – but of information! The ancient musty books and scrolls that lined the walls of the study rivalled those that Race had seen in the British Museum. Tomes of every language, from Portuguese to French to Arabic, were stacked on scarred wooden shelves, giving Abdulrahman access to secrets many a man would think long buried.

The Arab man smiled. "I see you appreciate my humble collection."

"My dear sir!" Race exclaimed. "Of course! I can only guess at the wealth of knowledge contained within this room."

Even Jaq was smiling, although to her most of what lined the walls was all Greek. She could speak English with the best of them, and was as fluent as the locals in Arabic, but she'd never been one for books or ancient scrolls. Yet, Race's enthusiasm was catching.

"How did you get all of this?" Race continued, walking along the shelves, his finger hovering an inch away from the books.

"Some of it has been in my family for years. Others I have picked up here and there. I am no scholar, Doctor Race, but my love of history makes me seek out information."

"I told you he was a good egg," Jaq said. "Queer, but good."

Race nodded, at a loss for words. What he wouldn't have given to own even half of such a collection!

"Ah, I did not bring you in here merely to admire my books," Abdulrahman said.

The old man went to a shelf upon which was stacked a variety of labelled metal tubes, looked at the labels carefully, and pulled one free. He unscrewed the top to withdraw a rolled-up map, before spreading it out on the big table in the centre of the room. It was a representation of The Empty Quarter, with a dotted line sketched across it from North to South.

"I know this route," Race exclaimed. "Thomas crossed the desert this way."

Abdulrahman nodded. "Indeed. The first western man to do so. I was fortunate enough to be with him. Here," he said, indicating a cross on the map, "is where we found a road."

"The road to nowhere?" Jaq asked.

"Yes. A manmade road that Thomas theorised could only lead to Ubar. We didn't have the resources to follow it all the way, or to search for more, but with what I've read in your journal, this may be what you are looking for!"

"You were in the Bertram Thomas party?" Race asked.

"I was. Remember, Doctor Race, he may have been the first white man to do the journey, but many Bedu have criss-crossed that desert for generations."

Race blushed. "Of course... I'm dreadfully sorry."

Abdulrahman held up a hand. "You are not the first Englishman to assume such a thing. You will not be the last. My point is that this may well be the final piece of the puzzle. You wrote that the man 'felt solid stone underneath his feet', correct? Well, there is not much stone in the desert."

"Except for that road," Jaq said, leaning forward to study the map.

"Indeed."

"You know, doc, I may be warming to this whole lost city idea."

Race flipped through his notebook, finding the page he was looking for. He read it once, twice, then leaned towards the map. His finger traced the route from the location of the road to the camp that the Bedouin had brought the injured man.

"My God," he breathed, "this could be it!"

It took many more hours of research, and a lot of co-operation between the three, to confirm the routes that they were to take when they began their trek. Jaq paused every now and then to write something down, taking note of the supplies they'd need, the number of camels, how long the journey would take – she recorded it all, running complex calculations in her head from long years of experience.

When they hit a bump in their readings, Abdulrahman would pause, think deeply for a moment, then run to a shelf to grab another scroll or yellowed book. They referenced everything from ancient trade routes by the Portuguese 300 years before to Islamic texts from even earlier.

Together the three of them built a plan that would take them to the Atlantis of the Sands, and when they were done, their faces broke into beaming smiles that only hinted at the supreme elation that they felt in their hearts.

"I must confess," Abdulrahman said, "that even with my misgivings, I cannot help but feel excitement for this quest. I still advise against it, however, for I do not think we will find the riches you seek, Doctor Race."

"The Colonel is the one that wants the riches," Race said. "For me, discovery is riches enough."

"But money makes the world go round, don't it doc?" Jaq insisted. "Having very little has taught me that, that's for sure and for certain."

Abdulrahman gave her a look that Race did not understand the meaning of. Another sigh escaped the man's lips. It seemed as if the man communicated a lot through such expressions.

The rest of the time was spent going over the route and supplies list a few more times before every one of them agreed that they had covered every eventuality they could. It was long past the call to prayer by the time they were finished.

"Are you sure you will not accept my company as escort?" Abdulrahman said as they were about to leave.

Both Race and Jaq nodded solemnly. The subject, said the nod, is closed.

"At least take a weapon, Doctor Race?"

"No," Race said firmly. "Can't stand the blasted things."

Jaq rolled her eyes. "They saved your life earlier today."

"But not in my hands, Miss Van Alden."

The subject firmly settled, the two were ushered out of the fantastic mansion and into the bracing night air. A breeze was blowing in off the Arabian Sea, bringing down the already chill temperature of the air a few more degrees. Both Jaq and Race pulled their jackets tight against the breeze, a bright smile spreading across the latter's face.

"What's up with you?" Jaq asked.

"Excitement, my dear," he said, his voice thick with joy. "The thrill of the hunt!"

"Danger notwithstanding?"

"As unfortunate as it is, it gives credence to our theories that the city exists!"

They lapsed into silence, walking down the deserted, chilly streets. The soft, warm glow of lights from second-story windows bathed them in an orange glow. Jaq could feel the exhilaration radiating off the Doctor. To her, he resembled a race horse on the line, rearing to go. He was almost skipping along the pavement.

"Do you often get this excited?" She asked.

"Oh yes," he replied. "Always have. History is exciting to me."

"Even if it is long dead?"

He nodded enthusiastically. "Ever since I was a boy. Our library in the house was my favourite place to be."

"Library?"

"Indeed. Our place was," he paused, embarrassed, "rather big."

Pictures of Victorian and Edwardian English mansions flashed through Jaq's mind. Stately places full of Lords and Ladies, servants and butlers, with a stable outside housing the best thoroughbreds in the country.

Alright for some, she thought to herself.

"Father was part of the old crowd nobility," Race continued. "We didn't have very much money, but we had the house and the grounds. He died in the war. Shell hit his trench. Very quick, or so I was told. I was only a few miles away, myself. Holding the line against the Bosch at the time."

"You both fought in the war?"

"Oh yes. We'd have been given the white feather if we hadn't. We had some very brave ladies round our way giving them out like candy. Bad business, the war."

His eyes went distant for a moment, the excitement fading like a candle that had been briefly smothered. Silence fell across them, so thick that all they could hear was the gentle lapping of waves in the harbour, and the odd murmur of Arabic from an open window.

"But that's all behind us now, eh? Only good things ahead."

"*If* we find the city," Jaq said.

Race hopped around, putting his hands on her shoulders and looking into her eyes, taking her entirely by surprise. The happiness was back. He radiated with it, she saw, as it oozed out of every fibre of the man's being.

"We'll find it, Miss Van Alden. I promise you that we *will* find the Atlantis of the Sands!"

CHAPTER 12

The next few days were a blur of activity for the party as they arranged their supplies, weapons, transport, and the various other bits of kit that they'd need for their journey. Colonel Stanley had finally managed to convince the British Government of the importance of the endeavour, and they in turn, had convinced the Sultan of Oman and Muscat to grant them permission.

When everything was arranged, all of it was sent to Salalah, which was the town from which Thomas himself had departed. They had all agreed to follow his route until they discovered the road that he had mentioned upon returning from The Empty Quarter, then set out on their own from there.

Race had sent a letter to Thomas asking if they would be able to meet, but the man said he was too busy, and wished them luck on their journey.

Fortunately for everyone, there were no further attacks from any of the black robed ruffians. Jaq kept her eyes open the whole time, however, for she knew that the danger had most certainly not passed.

"They will come at us again, I am sure of it," she said over dinner the night before they were to leave for Salalah.

The others all nodded their agreement. She noticed an odd glint in Alsop's eye, as if the man was looking forward to a fight.

"The desert will have many dangers for us, I'm afraid," Stanley said. "I get regular reports of warring tribes in the area. I doubt the natives will be very happy to see a party of white men in their territory."

"I have dealt with the tribes many times before. So has Abdulrahman. But these others, the ones that attacked us in the streets. They worry me."

"I agree," said Race. "I have been accosted by these brutes twice now. They are unlike anyone I have come across."

"You sure you won't take a weapon, doc?" Jaq asked.

Race smiled. "Yes I am, Miss Van Alden. I'll let Abdulrahman, the Colonel, and yourself handle the shooting."

"Nevertheless, I have ordered five Webley revolvers and five of the latest Lee Enfield Rifles, the No. 4 Mk 1, as well as enough ammunition to see us through a small war," Stanley said. "Solid British armaments that will serve us well, I'm sure."

"I heard the No. 4 hadn't gone into production yet?" Jaq said. "How on Earth did you get hold of five of them?"

Stanley tapped the side of his nose conspiratorially. "A small batch was produced for testing purposes. I was assured by a very good friend of mine that it is an excellent rifle and had a crate sent here soon after they were produced under the pretense of testing them."

"It appears that we are well enough equipped for any eventuality," Race said quickly. "Let's just enjoy the rest of our meal tonight. We have to be up early tomorrow, after all."

It was a fitful night of sleep for all of them, with each dreaming of the city, its supposed treasure, their enemies, and the great expanse of empty sand that was the *Rub' Al Khali*. In the morning, they all appeared a little the worse for wear as they piled onto the boat that would take them to Salalah.

The journey took them only a few hours, as their boat skirted the rocky coast and headed for the harbor at their destination. Most of them slept, doing their best to catch up on lost rest, but Alsop remained on deck the entire time, gazing out at the ocean and jotting things down in his notebook.

The excitement built within all of them the closer they got to their destination. They could feel it bubbling away inside their bellies, could sense the adrenaline filling their veins. It was so all-encompassing that each and every one of the party was awake half an hour before they were due to stop.

Stanley had arranged for them to spend the night in the Sultan's palace, since Salalah was little more than a small village, the plan being for them to set out in the morning when they were fresh and rested. But none of them noticed that curious eyes were watching their entire journey. Eyes that were as black as pitch, yet somehow still saw.

"They are sleeping in the hotel, Karim," said the small spy. "We should attack them in their beds and slit their throats."

They stood in a darkened street a block away from the palace. Karim, who was the big leader who had tangled with the group of foreigners on two occasions, shook his head.

"No. We shall take them in the desert, where we have the upper hand. Our creatures will be able to do more damage to them out there."

The man looked worried. "But controlling the beasts can be difficult."

"You have missed much since you came here as a youth, my friend. We have gotten better at it. Now go, back to your post. Watch them and make sure they set out tomorrow as planned."

Karim melted into the shadows of the alley behind him. The spy lingered a moment, sure that he heard the sound of leathery whispers on the wind. A chill ran through him and he hurried back to the palace.

Up in the air, Karim smiled as the cool night wind caressed his face. In the morning, his enemies would wake and begin their journey. A journey that could only lead to their doom.

CHAPTER 13

Every member of the party was up before dawn to partake in a massive breakfast, after which they proceeded to the edge of town where a small camp had been set up to hold their supplies. As they approached, they could hear the grunts and growls of the camels that they would be taking on their journey.

Once at the camp, Abdulrahman and Jaq gave the party a quick briefing for safety reasons on what they could expect while travelling in the desert. They went over how the journey would begin, with Jaq pointing to the stunning, mist-covered *Jabal Qarra* mountain range that lay between them and the Empty Quarter.

Briefing over, supplies and camels were checked one last time, weapons and ammunition were distributed, and everyone mounted their chosen beasts.

"I never took you for a violin player, Miss Van Alden," Race said when he noticed the violin case strapped to the back of Jaq's camel.

She smiled at him and gave a look that he could not comprehend.

"You may have been right, Doctor Race," was all she said in reply.

But when they set off at the distinctive, slow, loping pace that camels were famous for, Race felt his heart swell with ecstatic excitement, all thoughts of Jaq's strange look forgotten.

Ubar, here we come, he thought to himself.

As they approached the mountains, they were all treated to a fantastic sight of natural beauty that few had seen. The early dawn light lit the mountains in a glorious orange glow, the austere rock shining brilliantly. Jungle trees wrapped in perfumed jasmine dotted the slopes, while thick strands of lianas snaked their way among everything.

Giant tamarinds could be seen growing thick in the valleys, while just ahead of the party and their camels, standing tall among the long grass of the downs, were massive fig trees whose leaves swayed in the early morning wind.

"Take a good look, gents," Jaq said, upon seeing their reactions. "This is the last piece of green we're gonna see for a real long time."

Race had not been to this part of Oman before, so all he could do was nod as he marvelled at the sight in front of him. Alsop was sketching as he rode, a great feat of balance that Race himself still had to acquire.

They trotted onward, into the tall, flowing grass, and soon they were heading upwards on rough mountain paths. Jaq and Abdulrahman were in the lead, Race just behind them, followed by Alsop, with Stanley and the pack animals bringing up the rear.

At the slow canter that they were going, the camel was incredibly comfortable to ride on. Race didn't feel like he was being jerked and jiggled around at all, giving him time to take in the spectacular scenery that surrounded them.

It was close to midday when the mist started to clear, leaving clear, unobstructed views of the valleys that lay hundreds of feet below them. Rivers snaked through them towards the ocean, as most of the rain that fell in Oman was concentrated on these peaks. As the mist disappeared, the ground itself became more slippery, and Race feared that the camels would slip, but they never did.

The animals were as sure-footed as ballerinas on a stage, never putting a padded-foot wrong. It was no wonder that the Arabs and Bedu loved them so. A horse would have been struggling. Their only negative points were their constant noisy vocalisations and their rather unfortunate smell.

It was amazing to think that they were in one of the driest, most arid places on earth. Just a day ago, Race had been walking through dusty, sweltering streets, the only hint of green visible being those potted plants that stood outside the hotel. But now, he was in what could only be described as paradise on earth. An oasis of living beauty in a land whose attractiveness was more desolate than green.

No words were exchanged among the members of the party as they rode. There was no need to talk, and each of them was either so lost in the spectacle that surrounded them, or their own inner thoughts, that they had nothing to say anyway.

Up and up they went, some parts of the path were flatter, others steeper, but they continued to head skywards. The mountains themselves were not overly tall, and it was not long before they were setting up camp near the top.

As everyone else worked on making camp, Race forgot himself, and wandered towards the watershed. He was eager to see what lay beyond this lush region, to discover what lay ahead of them all for the majority of their journey. It was not long before he caught sight of it, as he found that he stood on the border between worlds.

Southwards lay rolling green fields, thickets, and spreads of trees. He squinted and saw that cattle wandered the meadows, grazing on the abundance of grass that waved in the wind. But just a little ways North was an entirely different sight.

There appeared to be no life at all to the North. Just parched sands, barren rocks, and only the merest hint of withered grass. The wind had picked up, and Race could see the dust that it carried along the barren wasteland before him, as if a fleet of spirits were making their journey from one world to the next.

"That, doc," said Jaq, "is what lies ahead. Miles and miles of very little, except sand, rocks, and the odd hardy desert animal. Quite a sight, ain't it?"

"Indeed," Race said in awe. "The transition from one world to the other is so abrupt that I can scarcely believe it!"

"If there's one thing I've learned in my time on this here earth, doc, it is that the natural world is far queerer than many imagine it to be. We build our cities and our skyscrapers and do everything we can to hold the natural at bay, but at the end of the day, it is what is going to do us all in."

She clapped him on the shoulder before heading back towards the camp to get the fire going. Race stood a moment longer, gazing out at the stark beauty of the world that stretched before him, and wondered if they all had the strength to make it to the end of their journey.

Talk over dinner was sparse, mainly focused on the things that they could expect from their upcoming trip. The camels groaned and barked and swore in the darkness just beyond the light of the raging campfire. A cool wind drifted in from the desert, rolling over the mountains and making the fire splutter and spit.

Race looked out into the darkness that surrounded them. It was a blackness so complete, so all consuming, that he felt as if they floated in an endless void out of time and space.

He shivered. The skin on his hands prickly. The hair on the back of his neck stood on end.

The leathery whispers that he'd heard before had started once more.

CHAPTER 14

They came out of the dark like beasts from some incredible nightmare. So wrong were they, so unnatural, that it took Race's mind a minute to figure out what they were. All he could comprehend were a mass of fur, demonic faces, leathery wings, and their black-clad masters perched atop them, swords held high.

Bats! Race thought. *Massive, demonic bats!*

That was indeed what they were. Bats larger than a camel, being ridden by men who were letting out savage war cries and brandishing viciously curved scimitars. The doctor could scarcely believe his eyes.

Gunfire sounded from his left as Jaq reacted. She was the first to take action, but it wasn't long before Stanley and Abdulrahman had joined her, the crack of the rifles painfully loud in the night. The muzzle flash of the weapons illuminated the gruesome scene in flashes, like a child's horrific slide show.

Teeth.

Flashing steel.

Dark, evil eyes.

One of the creatures was coming straight at Race. He didn't hesitate, diving sideways towards the fire as the thing flew overhead. It banked, circling around for another pass, its rider screaming for blood.

But this time Race was ready.

He had pulled a burning log from the fire and jabbed it at the creature as it flew straight at him. The thing screeched horribly, its terror overtaking its rider's commands as it shot skywards at a sharp angle. The rider screamed as he came loose from the saddle and plunged towards the earth to land in front of Race.

The doctor was ready, kicking the man in the jaw before he could haul himself to his feet. Race grabbed the fellow's sword and turned to face the next attacker.

"Come on you blasted beasts! I'll show you what the English are made of!" Stanley shouted.

Race could not help the smile that touched his lips. Stanley's sheer bravado and national pride was like a relic of a bygone age, but it was infectious.

A bat that was attempting to dive towards Stanley suddenly found itself without a rider. The man having been taken by a surprise rifle bullet to the head.

"Us Yanks aren't going to let you get off easy, either!" Jaq said, racking the bolt of her rifle back home.

Her cry was answered by more terrible shrieks from the darkness, followed by words that none of the party could understand. But their spirit was clear. The leader of the assault had just given a rallying cry.

The fight was not yet over.

They sprung forth from the blackness, the bats shrieking, their riders screaming. Stanley and Jaq opened fire immediately, and Race saw one rider fall from his mount, while another rider's bat dropped out of view to tumble to the foot of the mountain.

The doctor readied his sword as one of the beasts bore down on him. He waited until the last second before stepping to the side and slashing at the creature's rider as the thing flew past. The man gave a yell as the sharp blade cut into the flesh of his left arm. He lost control of his bat and they both went careening into the darkness beyond the light of the fire.

Race did not have time to gloat over his victory, however, as something slammed into him from behind, lifting him clear off the ground. He experienced a feeling of weightlessness and saw the ground soar away from him, as he realised to his horror that he was being carried into the sky.

He thrashed his arms and legs, trying to use the sword to slash at the bat that was now carrying him, but to no avail. He was held fast, and with each passing second, he was getting further away from the earth. Behind him, the beast's rider was laughing in triumph.

The laugh was cut short by the crack of a rifle, however, and Race felt the man fall from the back of his mount. The bat, now without a master, shrieked in terror and fury. It changed its trajectory, angling itself downward at an angle and diving towards the ground. The doctor struggled against the thing's grip, still trying to use the sword to slash at the nightmarish monstrosity.

The thing screeched once more and pulled up just before it hit the ground. Race felt the talons of the monster release their grip. He found himself hitting the dirt in a cloud of dust, tumbling end over end towards the edge of the cliff, the sword still clutched in his hand.

Then he was weightless, his body flying out into the blackness beyond the edge of the precipice. His body acted entirely on instinct as his mind was too filled with terror to form coherent thought. The doctor jammed the sword into the ground just before he fell, wedging it into the dirt just enough to hold.

He slammed into solid rock, the impact driving the air from his lungs. Race just managed to maintain his grip on the sword. He looked down, but saw nothing except blackness. A dark void that meant certain death.

Race tried to pull himself back to safety, yet try as he might, he found that he did not have the strength to do so. He felt his grip on the weapon loosening and knew that his demise was imminent. Until hands, soft, yet strong, grabbed his wrists and hauled him to safety.

"Thank you!" Race breathed. "Dreadfully sorry for the bother."

"No bother," Alsop said with a grin.

Race lay on his back, gazing up at the star-filled sky and marvelling at its beauty. It wasn't long before he realised that he could no longer hear the sounds of battle. He raised himself up on his elbows to survey the scene.

His other three companions stood with smoking rifles as they gazed out into the dark, ready for action. A couple of dark shapes were scattered about, casualties of the fight. Race gazed at one for a brief second before his mind, still numb from near-death terror, kicked into gear once more.

He leaped to his feet and ran over to one of the shapes. He quickly checked the man out – the very same one that he had kicked in the head moments before. It was just as he had expected.

"This one's alive!"

The man's eyes resembled two black pools that glinted in the light of the fire. Race saw nothing human in them, just an empty darkness that seemed to stretch on forever. The man snarled and said something that Race did not understand as Jaq and Abdulrahman hauled him to his feet to secure his hands behind his back.

"What did he just say?" Stanley asked, taking a drink from a silver hip flask.

Abdulrahman's eyes widened as the prisoner repeated the sentence. It was a strange sort of a language, sounding more like a faint echo on the wind than actual words. So mesmerised was Race by the man's speech that he just sat and stared, mouth hanging open. Only when Abdulrahman fastened a handkerchief around the captive's mouth to gag him did Race snap out of it.

"It is an ancient language," Abdulrahman said. "One that is not of this world. Mortal man should not speak it nor hear it spoken. With it comes only darkness."

"Bloody nonsense," Stanley said.

Race remained silent, staring into the prisoner's eyes, the memory of that strange tongue fluttering around his mind. He shook his head to clear it and felt his senses return to him. He stood, somewhat unsteady on his feet, his head feeling light on his shoulders. Stanley gripped him by the shoulder.

"Steady there," he said.

Race could smell the stink of brandy on the man's breath. It helped drag him back to the real world and ground him in the present.

"I'm fine, really. Just that voice... Something about it."

The doctor looked up to see Abdulrahman's eyes on him. There was something in the old Arab's expression. Worry and something more, although Race couldn't place it.

"What are we going to do with this bird?" Alsop asked.

"Keep him," Jaq replied as she sat the prisoner down by a large rock. "In the morning we can question him. Hopefully, we'll get some answers as to who these damned people are."

"No one's going to mention the giant bats then, eh?"

"What bats, my boy?" Stanley replied, taking another swig.

"That's what I thought," Alsop said.

"I'll take first watch," Jaq cut in. "The rest of you, get some sleep. Especially you, Doctor. You're not looking too good."

No one argued with Miss Van Alden, since they were all tired. Race wanted to say something, but even he knew that he needed rest. He had no idea how mere words had had such an effect on him and his scientific mind was keen to find out, yet at the same time, his head still floated uneasily in the air, as if barely attached to his body.

As he curled up in his sleeping area once more, he couldn't help noticing that Alsop had maintained a firm grip on his notepad and pencil throughout the attack. It appeared as if the man had been sketching during the fight, and now he sat by the fire, feverishly scribbling away as he observed the prisoner.

Race had to wonder what kind of a man sketched while others fight to the death. The blighter had saved his life, however, and for that he was grateful. It did not make the reporter's eccentricities any less odd, though. The Doctor lay contemplating the American as his eyelids grew heavy and he finally drifted off into a fitful, sweat-soaked sleep.

High above the camp, hovering in a lazy circle, Karim's pitch-black eyes watched. Rage bubbled within him, rage at the audacity of the foreigners below. At their sheer disregard for the ground upon which they so boldly trod. And at the fact that his men and their beasts had been bested yet again.

Not only that, but the devious foreigners had taken a hostage! One of his own, a man whom Karim trusted with his life. He fought the urge to spit on their heads from above, knowing it would only give away his position.

His objectives were now twofold. And while the first had not changed – the destruction of those below – a second had been added. Karim vowed to rescue his comrade from the clutches of the outsiders, no matter what it took. He knew he would accomplish his mission. It was the will of his Lords in the desert.

The party had won a battle, no more. A mere skirmish. And Karim had not attacked with all he had yet. A smile stretched across his face at the thought of the men and beasts he still had under his command.

"Sleep well, devils," he said, "for it will be your last."

CHAPTER 15

Race awoke from a dream haunted by that strange, alien language he had heard their captive utter. His eyes popped open, and he gazed into the sky. The air was so cold that his flesh was covered in goose pimples. His breath fogged in the early morning air.

"Morning sunshine," Jaq said.

Race sat up and turned his eyes to her. She sat cross-legged by the fire, a steaming mug in her hand. She gestured to the pot that sat next to the blaze, and the smell of fresh coffee came to the Doctor's nostrils. He yawned and shivered.

"Bet you didn't expect the cold," Jaq said with a smile. "Mornings are the worst."

Around them, a thick blanket of mist swirled through the air, cutting visibility to only a few feet on all sides. Race could not even tell where the edge of the cliff was. He moved to the coffee pot to pour himself a mug, using it to warm his freezing hands.

"Last night," Race began, then fumbled for the words.

Jaq nodded. "Indeed. Giant bats. Men with pitch-black eyes. This expedition gets weirder by the hour. It's a good time to turn back, Doc."

"No!" Race exclaimed. "Not now, when there are so many questions that I want answered. For instance, why are they so determined to keep us from *Ubar*? How did those creatures get so big? None of my questions will be answered if we turn back!"

"Spoken like a true scientist," Jaq said. "Or an explorer."

"Good morning my friend!" Abdulrahman said, clapping Race on the shoulder.

The big man sat next to Jaq and poured himself a cup of coffee.

"How do you like my coffee, Doctor?"

Race had to admit that it was a fine brew, better than any he had ever tasted. Abdulrahman smiled at this.

"It is an old family recipe, passed down from my father, and his father before him."

"It is delightful," Race said. "And what of our prisoner?"

"He was quiet all night. I think he knows that his friends will come for him sooner or later, so he has no reason to worry."

"Do we?"

"Have reason to worry? Always, Doctor. In this land, death can come from anywhere or anything. These madmen are only one of the things we have to fear."

"A comforting thought," Race said, staring out into the churning mist.

"This isn't the trip for comfort, Doc," Jaq cut in. "Comfort is a thousand miles on a boat the other way."

"You two seem so used to this kind of thing."

Abdulrahman laughed. "Miss Van Alden and I have been in a few tough places in our time. I have known her for many years, since she was only a girl. She used to be so reckless that I spent my life saving hers."

Race could have sworn he saw Jaq's cheeks colour.

"Last night you seemed troubled by our prisoner's words?"

The smile left the older man's face. "Yes, and I still am. But what can we do? We must take precautions. Worry will get us nowhere."

"Do you think he will tell us anything?"

"That depends, Doctor."

"On?"

"How we ask him the questions."

The prisoner was still seated in the same position he had been the night before, his back against the rock and his legs out before him. At some point during the night, he'd been covered with a blanket to keep the chill from getting to him. His black eyes watched them as they approached.

Alsop sat five feet away, scribbling away in his notebook. Race looked over the reporter's shoulder to see a very detailed sketch of the captured man that was so accurate it could almost have been a photograph.

"He ain't been moving at all," Alsop said, closing his notebook. "Just sitting there staring at me."

Abdulrahman crouched on his haunches a foot away from the man and spoke to him in Arabic. The man said nothing, just continued to stare with those soulless eyes of his. Abdulrahman repeated his question.

"I doubt he'll talk, old boy," Stanley said.

He walked over with a cup of coffee in his hand and stood, returning the gaze of the captive.

"I asked him some questions while I was on watch," the Colonel continued, "and I got no reply whatsoever. Whoever this chap is, he's very patient."

"Do you think you could make him talk, Colonel?" Abdulrahman asked, looking up at Stanley.

A prickle of revulsion crept through Race's insides.

"What do you mean, *make him*?" He said.

Stanley continued to stare at Abdulrahman for a moment, then looked away, his cheeks flushing. He used his free hand to remove the flask from his pocket and poured a measure of brandy into his coffee. He drank deeply, then answered the question, still looking down at the ground.

"I don't–" Stanley began.

"Come now, Colonel," Abdulrahman said as he stood, "I know you are capable of getting this man to talk."

Race looked at Stanley and was surprised to see the look of shame on the old Colonel's face. He bore a look of such ignominy on his features that it was as if he were a different man entirely.

"I don't do that kind of thing anymore. I refuse to," Stanley said at last.

Jaq put a hand on Abdulrahman's shoulder. "Leave it be."

Abdulrahman nodded. "Very well. I suppose I will have to try something, then."

"You will do nothing of the kind!" Race exclaimed.

Abdulrahman gave the Doctor a look.

"You think I'm stupid? I know you speak of torture, and I refuse to let it happen to any man under my care. And as my prisoner, this man is under my care."

"He wouldn't hesitate to do it to you, Doctor."

"Be that as it may, I refuse to lower myself to that level."

"That is rich, coming from a British man," Abdulrahman said, an edge in his voice.

Heat rose to Race's cheeks, yet he stood his ground.

"I... I cannot be responsible for the actions of my countrymen or my government, but I can control my own. While we have this person in our custody, there will be no harm done to him."

An uncomfortable silence descended on the group, which the stranger watched with interest. Stanley said nothing, simply stood and sipped at his brandy-laced brew. Abdulrahman studied the Doctor carefully, as if examining him for the first time.

"He will tell us nothing then," the Arab said. "We will get no information on what dangers await. We will have no idea how big the enemy force is. The expedition will be at risk. Are you willing to take that chance, Doctor?"

"I am," Race said, without hesitation. "And if none of you are willing, then I shall go alone. I will not be an accomplice to brutish measures just to extract information."

Abdulrahman smiled. "Very well. You know, for an Englishman, you are a surprising fellow."

"I can interrogate him," Jaq said. "I might be able to get something from him, without having to resort to violence. Do you agree, Doc?"

Race nodded. The tension broke suddenly, as if blown away on a gust of wind. Abdulrahman came over to shake the Doctor's hand. Stanley moved to his side soon after the man went to converse with Jaq about how to question the prisoner.

"Good choice, old man," the Colonel said. "That kind of thing... it... It never leaves you. Never."

And with that, he walked over to the fire and sat before it with his mug. Race looked at the old military man. He seemed defeated and tired suddenly, with sagging shoulders and a drooping moustache, his eyes glazing over as he stared into the smouldering embers of the fire.

CHAPTER 16

"This Doctor is not your typical Englishman, is he?" Abdulrahman asked.

Jaq shook her head thoughtfully. "No, he isn't. It's very interesting."

"Indeed. And it seems I misjudged the Colonel too. Perhaps this expedition will be more interesting than I thought at first."

"You don't like the English, do you?"

Abdulrahman shook his head. "I am fine with most of them, but their government hasn't been known to be very good to my people. Or any people, really, from what I have heard from my travels in India."

"That's why we kicked them out of our country."

The Arab laughed a deep, throaty laugh from the centre of his chest that seemed to cause the mists around them to swirl. Once he was done, he nodded, tears in his eyes.

"I hear the Indians are trying that," he said.

Jaq nodded, her eyes studying the prisoner.

"You think you can make him talk?" Abdulrahman asked.

"Maybe. I shall try."

Her friend nodded and placed a reassuring hand on her shoulder. He squeezed, then moved back towards the fire. After a moment, Jaq crouched in front of the captive, and reached up to remove the gag. She pulled it down carefully, continuing to keep eye contact with the man.

He sneered at her, lips curling up to reveal pure white teeth. His face was heavily lined and leathery, the kind of appearance one gets from spending their lives in the desert.

"I've seen and been called worse by tougher men than you," Jaq said, "so let's skip the insults, huh?"

More of the bizarre language flowed from the man's lips like water from a bottle. It was as if the air became heavier and the mists closed in around the pair, isolating them from the natural world.

"I don't speak your language, I'm afraid, but I know you speak mine. I can see the understanding in your face. If you're cursing me, don't bother. I'm already cursed."

Jaq tried to ignore the prickling at her neck as he continued to talk. But she remained silent, just watching him carefully, waiting for him to stop. Sometimes patience was the best way, and Jaqueline Van Alden could outlast many a person.

Eventually, the man stopped talking, his features twisting into a look of confusion. Jaq noted the reaction, filing it away in her mind for later as an interesting titbit of information.

"We done?" She asked.

The prisoner chuckled. "I suppose that I am, Miss Van Alden."

Jaq did not react to her name. Not a muscle on her face twitched.

"You're very polite, that's great," she said. "What do I call you?"

"It does not matter what you call me. The outcome of all of this will be the same. You and the other outsiders should turn back now. Give me the book. Walk away. While you still can."

"Can't do that, I'm afraid. But how about we let you go, and you call off your comrades?"

"So you can steal our treasures? Pillage our land?" He snorted. "Why would I do that?"

"Because we are not here to steal. We are here to discover. You see that Doctor over there? By the fire? He's not your typical explorer. And neither am I."

"You expect me to believe you? Foreign devils have taken so much from this land. But we have been here for longer than any other, and when your bones are but dust on the sand, we will still be here."

"Who are 'we', exactly? Bedu?"

"No, we are not of that travelling race. Nor are we of the people that now inhabit the cities. We are older and more noble. Purer than any of them. And we will keep our purity, as we have done for a very long time. No matter who has to die."

"I suppose that is a threat?"

The man nodded, grinning still.

"It takes a brave man to threaten his captors. I respect bravery, even when it borders on the foolish."

"*You* are the foolish ones. Death is coming for you, Miss Van Alden. It comes from the dark of the earth to drag you into its embrace. And unless you let me go, there is nothing you can do to stop it."

CHAPTER 17

"I take it he's not cooperating, then?" Stanley said.

The coffee was finished, and he was doing his best to rinse the last dregs out of the kettle. All of them were seated by the dying fire once more. All except Abdulrahman, who had volunteered to watch the prisoner.

Jaq shook her head. "It seems his companions are determined to keep us out of what he calls 'their city'."

"Ubar was destroyed centuries ago," Race said. "It's not possible that anyone still lives there. We would know by now if there was another settlement in the desert, surely? No one can be self-sufficient in the *Rub' al Khali*."

"He seems to be telling the truth, Doc. Which is why I'm worried. Because he's convinced we won't make it there alive."

Race looked over at the man. "Confident sort of fellow for one in his position, isn't he?"

"That's what I said. I'm guessing there are a lot more of them out there."

"So, we're up against an overwhelming enemy force?" Stanley cut in. "Sounds like fun, by Jove! What we British are best at, hey Richard?"

"We're not all English here, Colonel," Race replied. "But all the same, I'm not backing down. Not because some thug threatens me."

"Good show, old boy. Me neither!"

Jaq nodded. "I don't think we can go back now, anyway. I'm sure these people will hunt us down and slit our throats in our beds, no matter how far we go. Forward is the only way. Come on, let's pack up. We need to get moving before the damn temperature starts to rise."

They untied the feet of the camels and loaded up their stuff. The chill was starting to seep out of the air as they mounted up to begin the slow trek down the mountain path. Race was immediately reminded of how uncomfortable a beast his camel was when he was back on top of it. The thing snorted at him as if agreeing that it wasn't the best situation for her either.

With his back against the rock, his hands and legs tied, the prisoner glowered at his enemies as they got ready to leave. It had been decided that the best thing was to leave the man at the camp so that his comrades could get him at some point. They didn't have the supplies or the energy to keep a constant guard on a hostile man.

Soon, the party was meandering downwards, the endless expanse of featureless desert dunes appearing through the mists like some fantastic vision. The sand itself seemed to glitter in the early morning sun, the dew drops giving the impression that it was covered in diamonds. It was enough to take Race's breath away.

Jaq saw the expression on the Doctor's face and smiled. It was one of the reasons she had chosen to be an explorer. Looks of such wonder only happened when seeing something one had never seen before.

But something was nagging at Jaq Van Alden.

She knew that although the desert looked peaceful and empty, their enemies were waiting out there somewhere, with access to modern weapons and otherworldly creatures. Danger lurked amongst the sand, more than she was used to.

Casting a glance over the party, she found herself wondering how well they'd hold up. They'd all shown to have mettle when they'd been ambushed on the mountain, but this was just the start of the journey. She knew from first-hand experience that the longer you travelled through such a harsh environment, the more your morale dwindled.

Could they take the strain?

Jaq wasn't so sure. Stanley kept sneaking little sips from his flask. Race had already shown that he had firm moral convictions. And as for Alsop, she had no idea.

The reporter rode his camel with the easy grace of a seasoned hand, even going so far as to be able to sketch from atop the great, stinking beast. Yet he had not helped during the fight, and that bothered Jaq.

"So, what's it like being a reporter in this part of the world?" Jaq asked, bringing her camel up behind Alsop.

He paused in his sketch to look up at her. "Same as any other, really."

"But I would have thought New York or Chicago would be more your style? I've heard stories about men like Capone causing all kinds of trouble."

"Not all us reporters like that kind of action, Miss Van Alden." He spread his hands as if to take in the whole environment around them. "This is more my kind of thing. Let them birds in Chicago Land revel in the blood and bullets. This is where the real adventure is."

Jaq nodded. "I know the feeling. I never felt quite comfortable in cities. New York is quite melancholic after a time."

"You ever thought about putting your adventures to page?"

"My memoirs, you mean? No, can't say it ever crossed my mind."

"If it ever does, I'd be happy to write them. I'm sure this little adventure will be a big part of them."

"You think this will make us, then?"

Alsop smiled. "I think this will do much more than that, Miss Van Alden. We're going to find a lost wonder of the world, you mark my words."

"How can you be so sure?"

Alsop's eyes glinted as the sun's rays caught them. He touched the side of his nose.

"Trust me. I know."

CHAPTER 18

The first day of travel was uneventful and easily summed up in one word – hot. Sweat flowed off their bodies in tiny rivers, soaking through their clothes. It was made worse when Abdulrahman said the camels needed rest and made everyone dismount.

Race found the soft sand incredibly hard to walk through. In some places, it was as difficult as fresh snow. His feet sank deep into the dunes as he struggled his way upwards and over. Jaq, Abdulrahman, and even Alsop, made it look easy, but both Stanley and the Doctor had trouble. The wind that swept across the sands was little help, as it was like they were being blasted in the face by a furnace.

The Colonel's condition bothered Race quite a bit. The man's face had taken on a red colouration similar to a tomato, giving him a somewhat comical appearance of a sweating fruit with a moustache. At one point, Race had to stop the man to check his pulse.

"Nonsense!" Stanley had exclaimed. "Fit as a fiddle, as always!"

Race shook his head at the man's bluster as he strode forward with his head held high. As admirable as it was that he did not want to cause a fuss, it was infuriating for Race as a physician. He kept a wary eye on the man throughout the rest of the day, taking it off of him only when the sweat from his forehcad blinded him temporarily.

By the time dusk fell, Race was just happy to stop moving. It was a struggle to unpack and tie his camel, but once that was done, he collapsed onto the soft sand with a contented sigh. So tired was he that he didn't even notice the collected heat from the day burning through his trousers and heating up his rear.

"You going to help us make camp or just sit on your ass, Doc?" Jaq asked.

Race sighed, embarrassed at how out of shape he was. He'd been one of the most capable men in his regiment in the army, but now, he'd just proven to himself that that wasn't the case anymore. He hauled himself to his feet to help the others.

"Sorry," he said as he helped Jaq pack and get the fire going.

She shrugged. "Don't mention it. This place can be hard on those who aren't used to it. My first time out here was much the same."

"You seem like a local now."

"I was born to be out here. There's just something about it that speaks to my soul."

Race looked out into the ever-darkening horizon. "I suppose there is a certain majesty to all of this, lifeless as it is."

"Oh, it isn't lifeless. Believe me. Look close enough and you can find all kinds of creatures thriving in this place. I think that's what I like most about it. Man thinks he can conquer everything. The land, the oceans, the sky. But take away everything we have – all our industry, and we can scarcely make it a day in a place where a lizard the size of my pinkie spends their entire life."

"When you put it like that…"

"See?" Jaq said, grinning. "There's a kind of beauty that you can only find out here. A simplicity in it all. It's why I love the Bedu way of life. No cars or fancy houses or cities filled with people. Just a small group travelling across this vast expanse of sand. None of all the modern complications that we live with."

"Wouldn't they look at our supplies with disdain?"

"Of course they would!" Jaq laughed. "But how else am I going to get you English through this inhospitable place?"

"Not all of us are that bad."

She patted him on the shoulder. "You shouldn't take things so personally, Doc."

He nodded and said nothing. The rest of the night passed without incident, although Race was surprised at how fast the temperature dropped once night had fallen. The fire was barely able to keep him warm, forcing him to wrap a thick blanket around himself as he ate.

The others seemed in good spirits, but he couldn't get rid of the nagging feeling that something was wrong. A little voice in his mind was hopping up and down, trying to get his attention, yet he couldn't for the life of him figure out what it was trying to say. He kept attempting to grab onto it, to make it tell him its secrets, well past when everyone else had gone to sleep. Which was why he was wide awake when he heard the whispering.

Race sat bolt upright, his ear prickling as the murmuring came in on the wind. It wasn't words that he knew. They were strange and formless, a language he couldn't decipher, and it bore a resemblance to the one spoken by their prisoner. It was faint, as if being spoken from a great distance away, yet at the same time Race could hear it as clearly as if it were being spoken into his ear.

He stood, wrapping his blanket around him, and walked to the edge of the fire's light to peer out into the blackness. He strained his ears, hoping to catch some word or phrase that he could recognise, so that he could translate this strange, alien tongue.

"You hear it too?"

Race almost leapt out of his skin when Abdulrahman spoke. The man was on watch, and had approached the Doctor so silently that he hadn't even noticed until he was right behind him. A smile played on the Arab's face at the Doctor's reaction.

"I...," Race started, getting his heart rate back to normal, "I don't know what I hear."

Abdulrahman nodded. "Neither do I. It is a faint sound, although I fear we are heading towards it."

"Have you ever heard this before on your travels?"

"No, never. But I don't think they cared to let me hear it before tonight."

The night appeared so thick that it was as if the Lord Himself had put a blanket over the whole camp. No stars shone and no moon could be seen.

"I remember, when I was young, one of my friends kicked a nest of hornets," Race said, "we all got stung so terribly that day, even though we ran so fast. I feel as if we can't run from this nest, no matter how hard we try."

"Yes. We can't go back, Doctor, not now. Whoever these people are, they are fiercely protective of their ways and existence."

"And we know too much."

The two men lapsed into silence as the whispering stopped. It was just suddenly gone, like someone had pulled the needle off a gramophone in the middle of a record. Race looked up in wonder to see that the stars and moon had returned, their light piercing the ink black and giving life back to the night once more.

"Two things are certain, Doctor Race," Abdulrahman said, "these people are evil..."

He paused as something in the darkness caught his eye. Race turned his face to the man.

"And the other?"

"They are not of the natural world."

CHAPTER 19

YOU FAILED.

The voice seemed to come from everywhere and nowhere at once. It reverberated through Karim's body, shaking his very bones, and seemed as if it came from within and without his head. It was the voice of his Lord, and it was beautiful.

Karim was in the inner sanctum, where few of his comrades were allowed. As leader, Karim was afforded certain benefits, and direct contact with the Lord was one of them. The sanctum itself was dark, lit only by a hole in the ceiling where natural light filtered in.

AND ONE OF US WAS CAPTURED.

There was no emotion to it. It was just a statement of fact, as if it were saying that the sun would rise at the end of the night.

"We underestimated their effectiveness in combat," Karim said. "That mistake will not be made again. I have already taken steps to slow their progress."

WE KNOW. WE SAW THAT YOU SENT THE SERPENTS.

"Yes, my Lord. They shall reach the foreigners one night from tonight."

WILL THEY DESTROY THEM?

"I do not know," Karim answered honestly, for his Lord could spot a lie, "but it will be another obstacle in their path."

Silence descended into the dark alcove. Karim stood, waiting patiently, his head slightly bowed to show respect. Around him, the air was still, thick, and cloying, as if his Lord had His own atmosphere that He exuded wherever He was.

YOU ARE OUR MOST TRUSTED SOLDIER. WE KNOW YOU WILL STOP THEM.

"Thank you, my Lord."

Karim bowed and turned to leave, but the voice continued before he could.

FOR IF YOU DO NOT, YOU SHALL MEET A MOST UNPLEASANT FATE.

***

By the middle of the second day of travel, Race had adjusted somewhat to the demands of the trip. He found walking through the shifting sands easier as he learned to find his balance and not fight the walk. And even riding the camel, which protested and snorted and spat, had become a little more enjoyable. Sweat still poured off him like the rivers of the Nile, but that could not be helped.

Yet the Doctor's greatest concern was still Colonel Stanley. In Muscat, the man had seemed such a solid, dependable fellow. A big presence that could not be bent by even the strongest of gales. And now, he was reduced to a sweaty, red-faced man that hunched as he walked and spent every few steps gasping for breath.

He was still as game as ever, for the man was British Army to the end, but his body seemed to protest at every step. The drinking did not help, and Race found himself wondering how the man had made space for so much damn brandy.

"Stanley," Race said, coming up behind the man on his camel, "are you sure you're alright?"

The Colonel sucked water from his canteen before answering. Droplets dribbling down his chin and onto his already-soaked khaki bush shirt.

"Would you stop asking me that, man?" He exclaimed.

Race noticed that Jaq glanced over her shoulder at the outburst. He endeavoured to lower his voice.

"I didn't mean to offend you. It's just that I am worried for your health."

Stanley glared at him a moment longer before his eyes softened and he let out a deep sigh.

"Sorry about that, old man," he said, running a hand over his face, "I don't know what came over me. I'm fine, Doctor, don't worry. I just need some time to get used to being out from behind a desk."

Race nodded sympathetically.

"I'll take your watch tonight, old man," he said. "Let you get some rest."

The Colonel looked as if he was about to argue, but he seemed to think better of it. He nodded slowly, then set his upper lip, raised his chin, and urged his camel forward. Race watched him go, not knowing that he'd regret the offer he just made very soon.

CHAPTER 20

Race shivered and wrapped the blanket tightly around himself. The frigid air of the desert night was making his teeth chatter, while making it hard to stay awake. Abdulrahman's rifle lay next to him on the sand, and the sword next to that. He was in the third hour of his watch. Behind him, Stanley snored, a stark reminder of what the Doctor himself should have been doing.

Stars winked at him from above, but Race no longer cared to admire their beauty. What he wanted was sleep. He'd underestimated how much the trip was taking out of him. He stifled a yawn, stood, and did a slow 360 turn to look for any signs of danger.

As before, there were none, although the inky blackness made it hard to see very far.

Race sank to his backside again. This time a yawn escaped his lips, long and wide. He shook his head to clear the cobwebs, then heard a sound.

His head snapped sideways towards the noise. It was faint, so faint that at first, he thought he was imagining things. He stood up, peering carefully, trying to discern any sign of intruders.

There was something there. Race was sure of it. His imagination couldn't be conjuring up something so real, could it?

Slowly, he bent at the knees to grasp the hilt of the sword in his hand. Race would be damned before he used a gun again. The noise was becoming clearer now. It was as if something was sliding gently across the sand, the sound resembling running water in a stream.

Race took a careful step backwards, intending to wake the others. This was no hallucination, this was real.

Something was out there, and it was heading straight for the camp. But it did not give the Doctor the chance to rouse the rest of the party.

Something exploded out of the ground in a spray of sand a mere five feet away from Race. The shock of the thing's entrance forced the Doctor to take a step back that he misjudged, and he found himself falling. Something was rising out of the desert sands, something huge and hissing.

Grit rained down upon Race like rain from a dry heaven, and the creature's eyes shone in the moonlight. It turned its great arrow-like head towards him and bore its fangs. With an ever-growing sense of horror, he realised what it was.

"Snake!" Race screamed. "Great big bloody snake!"

The beast turned its glowing eyes towards him, hissed, and struck. But Race was already scrambling backward across the ground like a crab, sword still gripped in one hand. The thing hit the sand mere inches from the Doctor's feet in an explosion of grit that got into the man's eyes.

"Kill it then," Stanley grumbled.

Blinded, Race continued to shout warnings to his companions. He let go of the sword and used his hands to drag himself towards what he thought was the direction of his canteen. As he did so, he heard another one of the beasts slithering and hissing out in the darkness.

Expecting death at any moment, Race continued to claw his way forward. When something grabbed him by the shoulders and dragged him across the sand, he let out a high-pitched scream of pure terror.

"Relax, Doc," Jaq said in his ear, "it's me! Open your eyes and tilt your head up."

The Doctor did as he was told and felt cool water pouring onto his aching eyeballs, giving him sweet relief from the stinging. Around him, he heard the others rousing themselves. Stanley was swearing and Abdulrahman was shouting.

"There's two!" He roared. "Where's my rifle?"

"Take mine," Jaq yelled back. "Doc, take this."

She pushed the canteen into Race's hands. His vision had already begun to clear, and he tried to take in the scene while blinking furiously. Someone was already shooting, the harsh crack of the rifle followed by the tell-tale sound of the bolt being racked back. The hissing had intensified, and Race could sense, rather than see, the humongous reptiles slithering around the camp, waiting for the right moment to pounce.

"I can't see the bloody things!" Stanley screamed.

"Under the sand! They're under the damn sand!" Alsop said.

More gunfire cracked as Race was finally able to open his eyes. He was just in time to see a massive head emerge from the sand to hiss at the party. Jaq fired at it with her sidearm while using her other hand to drag her violin case from under her pack.

A tail whipped out of the darkness, sailing over the Doctor's head so fast that he barely had time to notice it before it hit Alsop square in the chest. The man let out a yelp and went flying out into the desert.

"Keep them busy, Stanley," Jaq said, getting on her knees beside her violin case.

"My pleasure!" Stanley roared.

He dropped his empty rifle and pulled the Webley from his belt. The thing barked loud and sent .455 calibre bullets slicing through the air towards their targets. One of the rounds struck their target, and the snake nearest Race hissed in pain as one of its eyes exploded in a geyser of crimson. The creature reared up and dove into the sand once more.

Race scrambled across the ground to his sword, grabbing the hilt just as something moved underneath him. He rolled to the side just in time to avoid the tail of one of the creatures as it burst upwards. As it came down, the Doctor raised his sword and stabbed forward, embedding the lethally sharp blade as deep into the flesh of the giant reptile as he could.

It thrashed in pain, sending Race flying. He sailed through the air, briefly weightless, before he hit Stanley and sent them both tumbling to the ground in a pile of tangled limbs.

"Get off me, man," Stanley said.

As the two of them struggled to untangle themselves, the thunder of automatic machine gun fire led them both to look towards Jaq. She stood, her feet apart and hips set, with a Thompson Sub-Machine gun in her hands. Race looked to where she was aiming and gasped as he witnessed the head of a snake obliterated into nothing more than mushy flesh and blood. It rained down upon the sand in a horrifically gory display.

She was about to swing her weapon towards the other snake when it struck at her. Race didn't even think, he just reacted, grabbing the woman by the ankle, and yanking her off her feet. The beast's great head missed her by mere inches and sailed on into the night, its lengthy body following like some demonic river of scales.

Instinct took hold of Race once more as his hand struck out to grab the hilt of the sword that was still embedded in the flesh of the snake. The Doctor suddenly found himself being dragged through the sand behind the creature, his mouth and nose filling with soil faster than he would have thought possible.

With almost superhuman strength, Race pulled himself up onto the creature's back as it slithered through the night. Behind him he could hear the cries of his companions, but their words were lost in the darkness. He grasped the sword with both hands while wrapping his legs as tight around the snake's body as he could and then heaved the thing blade of the monster's flesh.

The snake bucked him free almost immediately after, sending him tumbling into the night, still clutching the sword. The creature hissed and swung its mighty head around, its black eyes fixing on Race as he struggled to his feet, sand falling from him like water.

"Come on then, you stupid reptile," Race said through a mouthful of grit.

Without making another sound, the snake struck, fangs gleaming in the moonlight. Race was already moving before the creature had begun its attack, knowing that he wouldn't be fast enough otherwise. As the reptile's head slammed into the sand where Race had been standing, the Doctor was bringing the sword down on the thing's neck with a cry of rage.

Blood coated the sand and splashed all over Race himself, warm, sticky, and reeking of iron. The snake's head fell to the desert floor. Its body wriggled and writhed and thrashed in its dreadful death throes.

"Good show, old man!" Stanley exclaimed.

Race raised his blood-coated sword high.

"For King and country, you blasted beast!" He said, and collapsed into the dirt next to his fallen foe.

CHAPTER 21

The thing that awoke Doctor Richard Race the next morning was not the biting cold, nor the hideous sounds of some great beast, but the fact that he had no clothes on. His eyes popped open suddenly and he rand his hands across his body to ensure that he wasn't dreaming. The next thing to pique his interest was the aroma of fine, Arabian coffee that tickled his nostrils.

"Don't worry, Doctor," Jaq said, "I kept my eyes closed while I undressed you."

Race sat up and hugged the thick blanket around himself so that he could take the proffered mug of coffee from her.

"Why did you have to undress me?"

"Because you were covered in blood, and we did not know if any of it was yours."

Race nodded and took a sip of coffee. "So, it wasn't all some awful dream, then?"

"Afraid not. We can now add giant snakes to the list of wonders we have encountered."

The Doctor glanced around the camp. Everyone else still slept. A thick blanket of fog made it hard to see more than a few feet in either direction. And the air was so cold that Race's breath misted in front of him.

"Anyone else hurt?" Race asked at last.

"Not seriously. A few scrapes and bruises. Nothing major."

"And where did you get that Tommy Gun?"

Jaq smiled. "It was in my violin case. Never learned to play an instrument that didn't go bang."

Race nodded and drained the remainder of his coffee. His gaze shifted to Jaq, and when she didn't respond, he cleared his throat.

"May I get dressed now? It is rather chilly out here."

Jaq grinned. "No problem, doc. Meet me by the fire when you're decent."

Once Race had slipped into a fresh set of clothes, he took a moment to study the sword. It was a rather beautiful thing, its deadliness somehow enhancing its aesthetic, rather than detracting from it. And yet, Race could not help but hate it, as he hated all weapons. He'd seen first-hand what well-made weapons did to flesh and blood men during the war.

What he wanted to do was fling the thing out into the desert and forget about it entirely. But he knew that he couldn't do that. Not with the dangers that they now faced. And while he was still not able to pick up a gun, he could at least use the sword to help defend his friends.

He sighed and laid it next to his bedroll before striding across the sand to meet Jaq and the others. The sand itself cracked like glass beneath his feet, the chill having frozen the morning dew on the ground. Fog still swirled around him.

"Good job last night, Doctor Race," Alsop said.

Race nodded at the lanky newsman who was in his now-customary position near the fire, his notebook and pencil in-hand.

"Yes, jolly good show," Stanley agreed. "Although God only knows what else we have ahead of us. First giant bats, and now blasted serpents. Is this whole godforsaken desert out to kill us?"

"It does seem that way, yes," Abdulrahman said. "Perhaps *Ubar* is not meant to be found."

"You are a very comforting fellow, you know that? Blast whether it is meant to be found or not. We're bloody well going to find it! I just wish we didn't have to deal with the devil and his dammed serpents to do so."

"How much further do we have to go?" Alsop asked.

"Abdulrahman and I checked the map last night," Jaq said. "We have another three days of travel ahead of us."

"It's so close that it's a wonder the city wasn't found before."

"It probably was. They just weren't as good at survival as we are."

Alsop grimaced but said nothing. A hush fell over the group. It was only broken once Abdulrahman said that they needed to pack and get moving.

Once they were on their way, the camels grunting and snorting and jolting their innards, Race took his chance to sidle up next to Stanley. The Colonel had already started to take sips from his seemingly endless supply of brandy and was looking the worse for wear. Dark bags sat heavy under his bloodshot eyes, and his skin had the mottled appearance of a sick man.

Knowing that the man was sensitive to the topic, Race started to think of a way to bring up the man's drinking without offending him. Unfortunately, by the time the Doctor had come up beside Stanley, he still didn't have a clue what to say, so the two men ended up riding beside each other in awkward silence.

"I need it to function, old man," Stanley said.

Race was so taken aback that it took him a moment to understand what the man had said.

"The brandy?" Race said.

Stanley nodded. "If I don't have some every now and then, I start shaking. Conduct unbecoming of an officer, I should say. So, I keep myself in shape with the odd drink."

"You seem to be drinking an awful lot recently."

"Perhaps. Why do you think they sent me to Oman? Made a bloody fool of myself back in England, don't you know? A chap I know was kind enough to help me out under the condition that I don't do it again."

"How did you manage to get the go-ahead for this expedition then?"

Stanley laughed.

"I called in a lot of favours, old boy. Besides, I'm sure they don't expect me to walk out of this blasted desert alive." He took a sip from his flask. "And they'd love it if that happened."

Race eyed the older man. "Surely you don't mean that?"

"Oh, I do. I'm a bloody embarrassment to His Majesty's army, Doctor Race."

They carried on in silence for a moment. The sun was rising fast, the heat coming down so hard that it was as if the Lord Himself had turned up the oven dial. From atop their mounts, it was hard to see how anything could possibly live in such a harsh, unforgiving place.

"It all started in India, you see," the Colonel said at last. "Lovely country, India. You ever been? Bloody good food, and the people are some of the best in the world. I worked with those Sikh chaps more than once, and every one of them was strong as an ox. But the Indians didn't really want us there, Richard. Can't blame them, of course. Some of our lads were dashed unprofessional." He paused. "Sometimes, they were worse than that."

Stanley's features had taken on a melancholic quality. His eyes were unfocused, staring at something over the horizon that only he could see.

"I've seen things," the Colonel said, his voice distant, "and been part of things that I'd rather forget. When it was all over, I got a post in London. Started drinking almost immediately after I got back home. It got so bad that I didn't know whether it was night or day, at times. Conduct unbecoming of a Colonel in the British army, I'm sure you'll agree."

The older man wiped his eyes with the back of his hand. Race tried to think of something to say, some kind words of wisdom that would help the man, but he had none. All he had was a dry tongue and an empty mind.

"But that's in the past now, old man. I've been managing things a lot better than I used to."

"I'm glad, Colonel. However, I am still concerned."

"You bloody doctors always are. Relax. I will not compromise this expedition."

"That isn't what I'm worried about."

Stanley laughed. "Don't fear for my safety. You'd be the only one in the world who does."

"Hold!" Abdulrahman said from the front of the group.

Everyone pulled their camels to a stop. Race looked to where Abdulrahman had pointed to see a group of men approaching. They appeared to be Bedu, wearing flowing robes and wearing turbans around their heads.

"See that?" Abdulrahman said.

The one at the front of the group was kicking up sand in front of him as he walked. Everyone nodded.

"It means they're friendly. They probably want to trade. Everyone, get off your camels. Let's see what they want."

"Keep your weapons handy," Jaq put in. "But don't make any shows of aggression. There are laws in this desert that we must obey."

The leader of the group of Bedouin called a greeting in Arabic and Abdulrahman responded. The two met a meter in front of Race and the others before starting to chatter in rapid fire Arabic. Beside the Doctor, Alsop sketched furiously.

"Wouldn't a camera work better?" Race asked in a whisper.

Alsop shook his head. "I prefer the feeling of a sketch."

The exchange between Abdulrahman and the Bedouin continued for another minute, then Abdulrahman returned. He looked at Stanley.

"I'm afraid they need your camel for a moment, Colonel," he said.

"What? Blast them."

"Colonel, as Miss Van Alden said, there are laws. Your camel is a stud, which means it must mate with their female beasts."

Stanley's face took on a look of such horror that Jaq burst out laughing. He opened his mouth but no words came out.

"I'll take that as a yes, then," Abdulrahman said with a smile.

He took the reins of the animal and led it towards the Bedu. In a few exceedingly awkward moments, the deed was done, and Abdulrahman was on his way back with Stanley's stud in tow. The Colonel still hadn't spoken, and his face had taken on a bizarre shade of beetroot red. Jaq was still smiling, but Race noticed that Abdulrahman's face was deathly serious.

"I just got news from the Bedu," he said. "We're walking into an ambush."

***

Karim's eye started to twitch as he got the information from his scouts. The serpents had not even managed to thin the ranks of his enemies, meaning that he had invested far too much time, energy, and resources to get nowhere. The foreigners were not only proving to be more resilient than any who had come before them, they were also proving to be more resourceful.

He considered his options as the dawn's early rays peeked through the morning mists. There weren't that many. Every passing hour saw his enemies get closer to *Ubar* and brought him closer to the wrath of his Lord. He had already put a backup plan in place should the serpents fail, yet after that, if they survived, what then?

Perhaps there was only one alternative. One path for him to take that would ensure that the party would meet their doom at his hands.

Karim stood, dusted off his robes, and started towards the inner sanctum. He had something to discuss with his Lord.

CHAPTER 22

"Bandits?" Alsop asked.

Abdulrahman nodded. "That's what the *Bedu* told me. They spied tracks and signs of a large group of men. One of their number went to investigate, and it appears that they are lying in wait. I can only assume that they are waiting for us."

"I don't see who else they'd be waiting for out here," Jaq said. "How many?"

"At least ten men, armed with rifles. About a day's ride from here."

"Can we go around them?" Race asked.

"We can, but there's no telling how far around we'll have to go, and it would set us back a fair bit."

"What do we do? We can't just go through them."

"Why not?" Jaq hefted her Tommy Gun. "It probably won't be that hard."

Abdulrahman gave her a look. "We're not going to attempt to take them head-on. Especially after what happened two years ago."

"We survived, didn't we?"

"Only barely. And I couldn't hear anything out of my left ear for a week afterwards, Jaq."

"Then we must go around," Race interjected.

Jaq was silent a moment, gazing out at the sands. "Perhaps. But maybe there's another way that doesn't involve a full-frontal assault. Were the *Bedu* sure that these were ordinary bandits?"

"They were," Abdulrahman said. "Their scout recognised a few of their faces from raids."

"Then I think I have an idea."

Night had fallen by the time they came upon the bandit encampment. The bandits had chosen their position well, as it was surrounded by high dunes, meaning that they were well-concealed. Unfortunately for them, this also meant that they couldn't see who was coming towards them without posting sentries on top the very dunes that gave them cover, and Abdulrahman was the first to spot the men keeping watch.

"Everyone know what to do?" Jaq asked.

They all nodded, then, one by one, slunk off into the darkness until only Alsop and Race were left alone, lying prone on the still-warm sand. Race could feel the adrenaline coursing through his veins as he looked at his watch in the moonlight. Jimmy had a pair of binoculars to his eyes so that he could watch the sentries.

Race and Alsop did not have to wait long. One by one, the sentries stationed on top of the dunes disappeared from sight as Jaq, Abdulrahman, and Stanley carried out their duties.

"Well, I'll be dammed if they ain't gone and done it," Alsop whispered. "Even that old lush of a Colonel managed to take out a man without making a damn sound."

Race did not reply, instead focusing on counting sixty seconds using his watch. He wished he could be as flippant as Alsop, but there was a sliver of fear in his belly that was refusing to go away. What they were about to do was dangerous, and the more he tried not to think about it, the more it snuck into his subconscious mind to torment him. If he and Alsop didn't play their parts to perfection, then members of his party were sure to die, a thought that did not appeal to the Doctor in any way.

The second hand passed twelve on his watch face at last.

"It's time," Race said, rising into a crouch.

The two of them kept as low to the ground as they could as they crouch walked up the face of the dune. They stopped just near the top, dropped to their bellies, and bellycrawled the rest of the way to the peak.

Race peeked over the top to see the bandit camp below. About seven men sat around a fire, chatting, laughing, and eating. He took the binoculars from Alsop and took a closer look. That was when he saw that each man had a rifle either laid across their legs or on the sand next to them.

"You ready, Jimmy?" Race asked.

Alsop nodded and stood. The Doctor did the same and they both crested the dune and started down towards the camp, striding as confidently as they could on the incline. It didn't take long for one of the bandits to spot them and raise the alarm. Seconds later, seven rifle barrels were pointed squarely at their chests.

"Who are you?" One of the men barked.

He was a huge man, all muscle and hair swathed in a billowing robe. Even his rifle looked small in his massive paws, which gripped the weapon with an unnerving confidence. His voice rumbled from deep in his chest, a sound that resembled boulders rubbing together.

Race smiled at the man, who he presumed was the leader. "We're here to make a deal with you."

The big man laughed. "A deal? What kind of deal?"

"A very simple one. You pack up your things and leave, or else there will be trouble."

This time a few of the bandits laughed, evil grins spreading across their weathered faces.

"You look like one of the people we are waiting for," the bandit leader said, "they said you were brave. They should have said stupid."

Race raised a hand. A shot exploded out of the darkness and pinged off the barrel of the leader's weapon with a metallic clack. The man let out a yelp as he dropped his weapon. It landed in a puff of dust and for a tense moment, nobody moved. Race was keenly aware of the number of fingers hovering near triggers in his general vicinity.

"We have you surrounded," Race said at last, realising that he had been holding his breath. "Do as we say, and we will let you go free."

The big man's hairy head rose and glared at the top of the dunes, searching for some sign of life. Race could see the man's mind working as his brow furrowed and he considered his options. The Doctor couldn't help but pray that the man made the selfish choice, otherwise he and Alsop were just as likely to die as he was.

"I suggest you tell your goons to drop their weapons, or you'll be the first to die," Alsop said.

Race started to raise his hand, fearing that his thudding heartbeat was audible to everyone in the little basin. To his immense relief, the big man's eyes widened in sheer terror and his hand shot up in a placating gesture.

"Okay!" He said. "Drop your weapons! All of you!"

The bandits hesitated for a second, and then, one by one, rifles dropped to the ground in little clouds of sand. The men then stood there uncertainly with their hands hung awkwardly at their sides as they leader tried to figure out what to do.

"We will now go back to our men to say that you cooperated," Race said. "But don't think that we aren't watching you from the shadows."

Alsop and Race started to back up, careful to keep their eyes on the group of men as they did so. Race didn't start breathing again until they had crested the dune once more and slid onto their bellies on the other side. He slowly raised his head above the peak to watch the men below, once again praying that they chose life over death. He did not want another bloodbath on his conscience.

An argument had broken out among the bandits. A couple of the men were shouting at the leader and gesticulating wildly. One of the men bent down to scoop up his rifle. Another shot rang out and the argument stopped abruptly. A rifle cracked once more, this time from a different direction, and a bullet impacted near the leader's left foot. All the bandits looked at where the shot had landed, then after a few seconds, started to run around packing things up.

As the group of bandits raced about stamping out the fire and rolling up bed rolls, Race watched and thanked whatever Gods there may have been for their good luck.

"I can't believe that worked," he breathed.

Alsop smiled in the darkness. "This is all gonna make a helluva story, Doc."

Race was going to reply when someone screamed.

CHAPTER 23

There was an explosion of sand that covered a few of the startled bandits. Something moved through it at lightning speed, and suddenly, three of the men were swept off their feet and sent flying into the night. Someone had retrieved a rifle to fire blindly at whatever was attacking the camp, but they only succeeded in shooting one of their comrades in the head.

Race struggled to get a look at what was attacking, but whatever it was, was moving much too fast for the human eye to comprehend. A bandit's chest exploded in a gruesome blast of gore, causing another to scream and try to scrabble his way up the dune towards safety. Before he could, however, something snatched at his leg and dragged him back towards his killer.

"We should help them," Race breathed.

Alsop held him down and shook his head, his eyes gleaming as he watched the carnage.

More screams ripped through the night, followed by the sporadic rifle shot. Race watched, his mouth agape, his brain horrified and mystified at the same time. He had no idea what beast was killing the men.

And then, as suddenly as it had begun, it was over. As the cloud of dust settled on the still-bleeding bodies of the men, Race stared, still fighting the urge to race down the hill and attend to the dead and dying.

The Doctor had no idea how long he and Alsop lay there, waiting for the danger to pass before they could move. It was only when the two of them were almost scared out of their wits by Jaq as she tapped them on the shoulder from behind, did they realise that any time had passed at all.

"We need to move," Jaq whispered.

Together, the three of them slunk down the dune to find Stanley and Abdulrahman waiting for them at the foot of the hill, each of their faces looking just as queasy and drained of life as Race himself felt.

"Shouldn't we check on them?" Race asked.

Jaq shook her head. "They would have killed us all, Doc. That's what they were here to do. We can't risk our lives on the off chance we can save one of our enemies."

"Anybody know what that was down there?" Alsop said.

"Whatever it was, it came from underneath the sand," Abdulrahman said, "but I don't think it was a snake. It wasn't biting them."

The party had begun to move once more, heading back towards where they had left their camels and supplies.

"More like it was *stabbing* them," Jaq said.

She thought back to the scene. Whatever it was had moved so insanely fast, killed so efficiently, that none of the bandits had stood a chance. Even if their weapons had been in their hands, it was unlikely that they would have survived the attack. The whole thing had left Jaq with a hefty amount of respect – and fear – for whatever the creature was.

As they trekked back to their camp, everyone in the party kept glancing out into the night. Unease had settled over them like a blanket, making each footstep sound impossibly loud in the quiet. It was as if a curtain of dread surrounded them, as none knew what other seemingly impossible terrors the night could hold.

Jaq gripped her Tommy Gun tight, the weight and feel of the wooden grip against the skin of her hands giving her some comfort, some sense of control over the uncontrollable. A gun was one of the few things that ever helped her feel safe when she was pitted against the horrors of the world. She had learned from an early age that not all men were good, especially to women. Her father had known this and hadn't even attempted to shield her from the harsh realities of life.

But what they were facing now wasn't natural. It wasn't the kind of trouble she was used to, motivated by greed or lust and perpetrated by someone with no moral fibre. This was something else. Something Jaq was having trouble comprehending, and that scared her. She had dealt with greedy, unscrupulous, and lustful louts before, and could understand their motivations. Could figure out how to best them at their game.

These people with their massive, abnormal beasts and their eyes as black as night, she could not grasp so easily. And Jaqueline Van Alden was not used to being unsure. She was fast discovering that she didn't find it to be a pleasant experience, either.

"Damn and blast!" Stanley roared suddenly.

Jaq immediately brought her weapon to her shoulder, ready to blast whatever had caused the Colonel's outburst, then quickly saw that bullets would do her no good.

Something had gotten to their camp while they were gone. It was a mess, supplies strewn this way and that across the sands. Of their camels, there was no sign, except for a couple of discarded pieces of rope that lay twisted on the ground.

For a while, no one spoke, each surveying the destruction and keeping their dark thoughts to themselves. It was Alsop who eventually broke the silence.

"I suppose this could be a problem."

CHAPTER 24

The party carried out a thorough inventory of their remaining supplies, and the results were less than favourable. They piled everything salvageable into neat stacks, started a fire nearby, and sat around it, glancing at their remaining provisions every now and again, as if hoping for the pile to miraculously grow in size.

"We are okay for bullets and water," Jaq said, a cigarette hanging from her lips, "but that's about it. Our food stores were hit bad, as was everything else. The biggest loss was the camels. There's no way we can make it back to civilisation from here without them."

"Thank God I carried the journal and the map with me," Race said.

He had both open in front of him and was gauging distances.

"Look here," he said, "we can make it to *Ubar* from on foot. It will take us a day and a half."

"We cannot make it anywhere else," Abdulrahman said, gazing at the map. "I feel like we're being herded towards the city. Our only hope otherwise is to run into the *Bedu*."

"My thoughts exactly," Jaq agreed. "They can't stop us getting to their city, so they've probably laid a trap for us there. What better place to take us on than their home turf?"

Race rubbed his face with his hand and let out a heavy sigh. "I was thinking, after seeing what happened to the bandits, that it was time to head back and leave the city to its slumber. Now, however, it appears as if we have no choice."

"Even if we had one," Stanley said, "I wouldn't have turned back. We've come too far and shed too much blood to turn back now. I will make it to that blasted city, even if they kill me there. I'll stain their damned streets with my blood to spite the bastards, if I must."

"First things first," Abdulrahman said, "we ration out our provisions. Then we sleep and travel at dawn."

Everyone voiced their agreement. Alsop was the only one seemingly undaunted by the setback, and even offered to take first watch. Jaq disagreed, ushering the man to sleep once the rations were sorted, and took position at the edge of the firelight, her Tommy Gun across her lap. She craved another cigarette, but the light of it would give away her position, so she held off.

Outwardly, she appeared calm. Inside, however, she was less serene than her placid expression belied. The need for a smoke told her that. It was only when she was truly stressed that she craved tobacco. Otherwise, she could take or leave the things. Which was odd, since she remembered when it had first become fashionable for ladies to smoke in the 1920s, and she had been one of the first to take up the habit, much to the displeasure of her father.

They're dangerous, Jackie girl, you mark my words, he'd used to say.

She smiled at the memory and couldn't help but wonder what he'd make of her current predicament. She supposed that she would never know, considering how unlikely it was that anyone of the party was going to make it out of there alive.

Her neck prickled and she spun around, the Tommy Gun's stock on her shoulder. Someone was out there in the dark, watching them, she was sure of it. Their presence was undeniable, yet she could not see or hear anything unusual. The night sounds of the desert played on her ears, the place coming alive with all manner of tiny critters. Above the stars shone bright.

And despite the usually calming effect of nature on her person, a cold shiver ran down Jaq's spine.

She lowered the weapon, and scanned thick, impenetrable blackness that was only just kept at bay by the light of their fire. It was odd how the light of the moon and stars wasn't even making a dent in it.

No, she thought, *not odd. Unnatural.*

Dread crept its way around her spine and found her intestines, wrapping around them and twisting them into knots, causing pain in her abdomen. Instead of bowing to it, Jaq stood straighter, setting her shoulders back and her chin out. Whatever was out there, it would not find her cowering. If she was going to go down, she was going to fight tooth and nail, as she had all her life.

***

From a safe distance away, concealed in the blackness that his Lord had created for him, Karim watched the woman search for him. He was not worried – there was no way she could see him. Even so, when her gaze came to rest on his position, he couldn't help but feel as if she was watching him.

He could not help the smile that spread across his grizzled features. Although this woman and her party of invaders were giving him grief, he had discovered a respect for them. Most surprising to him, that newfound admiration was greatest for the woman. He could see the fear in her, could almost taste it on his tongue, and yet she stood up straighter, as if daring him to make a move.

As Karim had never had much respect for females, this was an interesting new development. He wondered if he and his brothers had been remiss in not letting the women of the tribe join them all those centuries ago. It was a moot point, but an interesting one for him to ponder.

He supposed that it did not matter how much the woman impressed him. In the end, she would die just like the other members of her party. *Ubar* was no longer meant for humans. Its soil was sacred, having been cleansed of the impurities of its sins long ago. Any humans that stepped within its walls were destined for destruction. Karim's Lord demanded it be so.

It was a bargain that had been struck many years ago, and one which Karim and his brothers were happy with. The rewards that they were given were too great. And they had been plucked from certain doom as their once-great city burned around them.

Karim was taking advantage of one of those rewards to watch the woman from the blackness. It cloaked him, covering him in its cold embrace like an old friend, keeping him safe from the prying eyes of his mortal prey.

He knew the party would make it to the city. That was fine, because there they would find Karim waiting for them. He and his brothers would be atop their great beasts, waiting for their prey to wander into their trap.

Ubar would be the grave of the small party of foreign devils, and no one would ever discover what had happened to them, as had happened with so many before.

CHAPTER 25

"I hope the Atlantis of the Sands is worth dying for," Alsop said.

The way he said it, not with any sort of grim foreboding, but with joviality, tickled the back of Race's hands. There was something wrong with the man, he was sure. He just wasn't so sure what it was.

They were trudging through the soft desert sands, their boots sinking with each footstep, as if it was snow that they were walking on and not earth. Their backpacks felt heavy and unwieldy, even though they did not weigh that much. The guns seemed to have increased in weight, too, the heat playing its tricks on their strength. Race was glad he didn't have a rifle, instead opting to carry the sword strapped to his waist.

Jaq was by far the fittest of the lot, with Abdulrahman a close second. As such, she was in the lead while he brought up the rear. Sweat poured off everyone's face, each droplet shedding more of their precious water into the uncaring sands. Every now and then, Race would see a lizard dart across the hot earth and disappear, and he found himself wishing he was that well-adapted to the harsh environment.

Their pace was measured, not too slow, nor too fast. Jaq had spent long months in the desert, surviving with very little, and it was the skills she learned throughout those months that she brought to bear then.

The Doctor found the figure that she cut as she led the party strangely alluring, and expected that if he had had a camera, he could have made a grand portrait of the woman. It was thoughts like these that kept Race going, as they took his mind away from the dreariness of the task at hand. It was his first time on such a trek, and as far as he was concerned, he would ensure that it was his last – even if he did survive it.

"You doing okay, Doc?" Jaq asked over her shoulder.

"Tickety boo, Miss Van Alden," he replied. "I must confess, however, that I am more used to cold weather."

"You know the best thing about the desert? At least your boots don't get wet."

"That is one advantage this place has over the trenches, I'll admit. But I am sweating so much that my socks are wet anyway."

"Can't help you there, Doc."

He laughed. "Wasn't expecting any. My thoughts are more preoccupied with whether we'll survive this, at any rate."

"We might," Jaq said with a shrug, "I've been in some bad places in my time. I'm still here."

"Only a few years ago, I was convinced I'd die in a muddy trench. I suppose life has all kinds of ways to kill us."

"I think you mean *Man* has all kinds of ways to kill ourselves."

"And yet we are not fighting men here, are we?"

"You may be right. But men have something to do with it, I'll bet. Whatever is behind these unnatural occurrences, we still find men alongside it, do we not?"

"I must wonder if those black-eyed people are still human anymore. Or just… people shaped."

"I think there's still enough humanity within them to be dangerous, Doc. Beasts like those snakes and whatever it is that killed the bandits don't just attack for no reason. They were trained to do so."

"You think Man is the only species capable of evil?"

Jaq nodded. "I do. I've seen a lot of it in my time. It's why I like this place. I can be myself here and no one will try and tell me different. I won't be told to wear a skirt, or be a dammed lady, or told how pretty I am. And I won't witness the evils of our species as often as I did living in New York."

"A few days ago, I'd have agreed with you, Miss Van Alden. But now, I am not so sure. I think something else is behind all of this. Something unnatural. All the tales I have read of *Ubar* say that it was destroyed by the gods for its hubris. Perhaps it wasn't any god that brought the city to ruin."

"You mean that we can tempt the devil just as easily?"

"Perhaps. Or perhaps it's something worse. Hopefully, we can find out what before it kills us."

"You know, Doc, you're a cheery sort."

He smiled. "I apologise."

"Don't. You don't have to. We all deal with difficulty in different ways. And at least you aren't doing what your friend Stanley is."

They looked back at the red-faced older man. It seemed as if he was truly struggling, with each of his steps seeming laboured and heavy.

"He'll get to the city," Race said.

"What makes you think that? He looks ready to drop," Jaq said.

"He has something to prove. Not to us. To himself."

Jaq nodded. "I'll trust you on this. But just so you know, none of us are carrying him there. We already have enough on our backs."

Race was about to reply, perhaps with some valiant defence of his countryman, but his foot touched something on the ground that made him look down in fascination. He stepped down in the same spot once more, harder this time, and was amazed to feel the same result beneath his tread. He swept his foot sideways to brush away the sand and stared down at what he had uncovered.

"What is it, Doc?" Jaq asked. "You step on a liz–"

The words caught in Jaq's mouth as she looked down, her eyes fixing on what was beneath Race's foot. She tapped her foot against the ground, then got on her knees and furiously swept the sand aside in a wide circle, the epicentre of which was where Race stood. The others watched in amazement as she uncovered part of a road.

The Doctor dug the journal out of his pocket and flipped through the pages desperately. He found the one he was looking for, his finger running over the words so that he could make sure that his brain was not tricking him.

"This is it!" He exclaimed. "The road to *Ubar*!"

It was, indeed, a road. Made of carved stone slabs and about twenty feet across, it was a marvellous piece of ancient engineering that had survived centuries of wear and tear.

"That way," Race said, pointing eastwards, "we are close. Very close."

He no longer felt the heat that pressed in around him, so excited was he about the find. His eyes gleamed.

"Let's hope this goes all the way there," Jaq said.

"It will. The journal says so."

"The journal of a madman?"

"He wasn't always mad. Only once he returned from *Ubar*."

"That's comforting."

"We must move," Abdulrahman said. "We can't afford to waste time we don't have."

"Agreed," Jaq said with a nod, "lead the way, Doc."

The party started moving once more, this time being careful to stay in the middle of the road, a vague outline of which could be seen under the sand, if one was looking carefully. Jaq kept close to Race as they went, with Alsop excitedly sketching in the middle, and the Colonel and Abdulrahman in the rear.

"You don't like me, do you, old man?" Stanley asked.

Abdulrahman shot a sideways glance at the old Colonel, at his bushy moustache and typically British get-up, a stark contrast to his own flowing robes and bearded, lined face. Even in the heat of the desert, with sand surrounding them, and not a single building for miles – a place as unlike England as one could get – the man was still unmistakeably English. It was if he was stopping just short of hoisting the Union Jack above his head and declaring that the Lord would bless his King and country.

"How can I like one who carries their country with them like a badge of pride?" Abdulrahman said at last.

"What?"

"Think of it this way. When I was in your country, I wore a suit and tie and polished shoes. Yet here you are, in my homeland, wearing what an Englishman would."

Stanley thought for a moment, his eyes dancing over the horizon. He let out a sigh before he spoke again.

"I am an Englishman, so I wear what Englishmen wear."

"Yet, when I am in your country or India or Africa, what am I expected to wear?"

"You don't have to."

"Don't I, Colonel? You mean they would let me into buildings in London if I wore my robes and didn't shave my face? You English, you go to lands that are not your own and you make them yours, no matter what the people of that land say. Then those same people are expected to dress, to act – to *be* – English."

"I…"

"And answer me this Colonel, what happens if they don't act English?"

Stanley said nothing.

"Come on, Stanley. I know you've seen what happens up close. Where is your English pride?"

The Colonel dropped his head. He pulled out his flask, but Abdulrahman grabbed his wrist, preventing him from drinking.

"You have seen it. I see it in your eyes. And you hide with it every day, with this," he said, ripping the flask from Stanley's grip. "You hide from the truth of the atrocities you have committed for your country by drinking."

Abdulrahman threw the flask out into the desert as hard as he could. It caught the light as it flew away, glinting briefly at the top of its arc before it fell out of sight.

"No, I do not like you, Colonel. How can one like someone who is less than a man?"

Stanley opened his mouth to talk, yet no words came. So, he shut his lips and nodded slowly. He quickened his pace to put some distance between Abdulrahman and himself. Abdulrahman watched him, his expression neutral.

Perhaps, he thought, *just perhaps.*

The walk turned out to be a lot easier on a stone road, and the party ended up making better time than expected. At nightfall, they were less than half a day from their destination, if all went well.

Alsop argued that they push forward, but Jaq was against it. It was agreed that they all needed rest, as none knew what they were going to face once they reached the city. Chances were good that there was going to be a fight. In the end, even Alsop acquiesced, and the party had a night of fitful sleep thirty feet away from the road.

And still they were up before dawn, aiming to take advantage of those precious moments of cool temperatures that occurred before the sun rose. They walked through the swirling mists, the sand cracking like ice beneath their tread, back to the road.

Once there, they all stood a moment in silence, knowing that it was the day that they would finally discover if the Atlantis of the Sands was, indeed, real. Whether it was worth the blood that had been spilled in pursuit of it. Even though he was struggling to contain his excitement, Race could not help but feel that nothing was worth the death and destruction that had followed the party in pursuit of this lost city.

After their moment of reverence, everyone nodded, and they resumed their trek. The road made the going easier, and every single member could feel their hearts beating faster as each step brought them nearer to their goal. The sense of anticipation was palpable, even more so than the heat that was slowly starting to creep its way back into the air.

It took them the better part of half a day, but finally, they made their way between two massive dunes, and there for all to see, stood the ruins of *Ubar*.

CHAPTER 26

All in all, it wasn't as grand a spectacle as they had been hoping for. No one exclaimed anything out loud, there was no overwhelming sense of wonder. Just a general feeling of disappointment.

The city itself was lying in ruins, half-covered in desert sand. If it weren't for the cover of the large dunes that encircled what was left of *Ubar*, race was sure it would have been completely buried. Stone pillars stood here and there, most leaning at weird angles, with crumbling walls between them. The road they were on seemed to be the main thoroughfare, leading directly through what Race suspected was once the middle of the city.

As the party stepped within the city's limits, Race noticed that the destruction around them seemed to fit a pattern. The walls and pillars and other remains seemed to get larger the closer to the outskirts they got, although it was hard to tell, since nothing except the odd pillar was taller than a person.

No one spoke as they made their way through the ruins, each processing the sight in their own way. Race had to admit to a tinge of disappointment, yet when he saw what was around him, and considered its age, he could not help but marvel at what had to have been one of the greatest cities of the ancient world.

"This can't be it!" Stanley exclaimed. "Where's the riches? The streets paved with bloody gold?"

"Long gone, it seems," Jaq said, running her hand gently over what was left of a crumbling wall.

"You mean to tell me those blighters we've been fighting were killing for *this*?"

Race ignored the man, instead casting his gaze about to see if he could confirm his theory.

"They weren't stupid, those men," the Colonel continued, "I doubt they'd have been so keen to keep us away if this was all there was."

The Doctor nodded to himself. Stanley was right. There *had* to be something else. Impressive though the scale of the ruins were, they weren't worth killing for. They were an incredible archaeological discovery and would make each and every one of their names in the right circles, but one did not kill to hide crumbling masonry – no matter how old it was.

"This is a bloody–"

"Shut up, you dammed English idiot!" Abdulrahman shouted, cutting Stanley off. "Can you not use your eyes? The Doctor has an idea, and if you'd be quiet for a little bit, maybe he could share it with us?"

There was a stunned silence and for a moment, the whistling of the wind through the stone was the only sound that could be heard. Stanley had gone red in the face from embarrassment, and instead of replying with bluster, instead bowed his head and mumbled an apology. Race was so engrossed in his thoughts that he paid no attention to any of this, and after Abdulrahman's admonishment of the Colonel, no one was going to say a word so that the Doctor could be left to his thoughts.

Race walked along the road, then down a side street, following the pattern of destruction that he had noticed earlier. The others followed behind him as he muttered to himself, stopping every couple of steps to kneel and check the floor, or lean in close to one of the walls. After which, he'd nod his head sagely. At one point, Alsop shot a look to Jaq, but she just shrugged, so he went back to his sketches.

The city itself was still immensely impressive, even ruined as it was. It was obviously designed with a plan in mind, with streets laid out in a logical manner, allowing for easy traversal through its quarters. The houses were well-made, with spacious insides that seemed well-laid out for the desert, suggesting the ancient dwellings that Jaq had seen in Egypt. Roads were large enough for carts to roll along, with ruts carved out of the stone giving an indication of where they had once ridden on a regular basis.

Eventually, Race led everyone to a part of the city that was made entirely of rubble, the structures in it having been destroyed in what seemed to be a rough circular pattern. The Doctor knelt, picked up a piece of stone, and tossed it to Jaq.

"What do you see?" He asked.

Jaq examined the rubble. "Scorch marks."

"Indeed. And where we're standing is the epicentre of the blast that destroyed the city."

"It does look like a shell landed in the middle of this place."

"You're saying this ancient city was shelled?" Stanley asked.

Race shook his head. "It was destroyed by the will of God, remember? For rising too high?"

"A meteor?" Abdulrahman said.

"Yes!" Race said with an excited nod. "The destruction emanates out from this point. I think a meteor landed here and destroyed the city. Look at how things are scorched. I noticed marks leading all the way back to the entrance to the city."

"So, what happened to the survivors? Did they just leave?"

"I think I found something," Alsop called from the middle of the clearing.

They all went to him and saw him kick something at his feet. It was a large, thick, stone that had been carved into a smooth flat circle.

"You know what this looks like to me?" Alsop said.

They all nodded. Alsop was the first to drop to his haunches and grasp the stone slab. The others followed suit, and on the count of three, heaved the slab forwards to reveal a hole beneath it. Everyone counted again and pushed once more, this time with more force, their muscles straining against the weight of the stone. It scraped along the ground noisily, the sound setting Race's teeth on edge, but eventually it started to move easier. It only took a couple more shoves to make a hole big enough for a person to fit through.

Jaq pulled a torch from her belt, clicked it on, and shone it into the hole. The light revealed carved stone steps leading downwards into a darkness so thick that the torchlight could only penetrate so far. As they gazed downwards, the wind picked up suddenly, carrying a cloud of dust over the ruins of the city and the party itself.

"Guess we're heading down," Race said, coughing as the stuff got into his throat.

The wind was picking up and they could see a massive dust cloud on the horizon. They had no other choice but to descend the steps into pitch blackness.

CHAPTER 27

Above them, the sandstorm raged, but inside the tunnel, the air was dank, with a foul stench wafting towards them from deeper within. Race shone his torchlight along the walls, letting out a gasp when he saw what was engraved upon them. Stepping closer, he illuminated a spot to confirm his suspicion.

"What is it, Doc?" Jaq asked.

She was on-edge, every sense she had telling her that there was great danger ahead somewhere. And something about the smell that surrounded them was bothering her, triggering an old memory that she could not quite recall.

"Look here!" Race said, pointing.

The walls were engraved with writing. It wasn't a script that Jaq recognised, with lines that wrapped back and forth along the wall in intricately carved patterns.

"I recognise this," Abdulrahman said. "It is called Safaitic and is very old. Ancient."

Race nodded excitedly. "Yes. From the 1st Century BCE at least! Can you read it? I can only decipher some of this."

Abdulrahman stepped closer. The runes were carved at various intervals along the walls on both the left and right sides. Race was hurrying from one side to another, running his light along the inscriptions that he found and scribbling in his small notebook, while Abdulrahman took things at a slower pace. As they read, they moved forward, down the tunnel until it reached a T junction.

Jaq noticed that the passageways were roughly carved into the rock of the earth but seemed well built enough not to collapse on top of their heads. Yet, she couldn't shake the feeling in her stomach that they were being watched.

She felt much the same as she had on that night keeping watch after the attack on the bandit camp.

"This way," Race said, heading down the left path.

Jaq pointed her light down the right passageway, trying in vain to penetrate deeper down the darkened tunnel, convinced she'd see the face of one of those men staring back at her. A glance over her shoulder told her that she was being left behind, so she hurried after the party, the grip of the Tommy Gun clutched so tightly in her hand that her knuckles were white and the wood bit into her flesh.

It was not long until the party came upon a large chamber, at the centre of which raged a large fire. The walls were a mass of runes, the Safaitic carved into the rock wherever a person could reach. Bedrolls were arranged around the fire, all of them old, and looking as if they hadn't been used in years. The same could be said for the rest of the pots, jars, and clothes that were piled up in heaps at random intervals along the walls of the space.

Race and Abdulrahman continued to examine the walls, starting on the left and going in a clockwise direction around the room. Not all of the writing was useful or relevant – some of it just graffiti, talking about women or needing sleep or wanting more supplies – but as they read the runes, the two men started to get an idea of what had happened to the city above. All the while, Alsop watched, still sketching by the light of the fire.

Meanwhile, Jaq and Stanley watched the tunnel that they had come from, both peering into the darkness, ready to be attacked at any moment. Jaq sensed that the Colonel had the same sense of danger that she did, probably because they weren't as caught up with the writing as the other three. Thus, it was up to them to ask the tough questions, such as the identity of the person who lit the fire.

"I think I know what happened here," Race said, looking to Abdulrahman.

The older man nodded. "As do I."

"Well, hurry up and tell us so that we can scram," Jaq said over her shoulder, "I feel like this could be a trap."

At Race's urging, Abdulrahman told the tale.

"It was a meteorite," he began, "it struck the city when it was at its most profitable. According to the writing, it was thought by the people of the city to be a punishment from God Himself because *Ubar* was living in sin. Only a few people survived, and they went to the meteorite the next day because it was glowing. It is said that the word of God came from within the rock, giving them instructions on how to live. The survivors were convinced that it was God who was talking to them, so they did as they were told. They dug these tunnels, and as they did so, they realised that they could see in the dark and that they no longer needed food or water. The more they did as they were told, the more miraculous their powers became.

Eventually, they were given the ability to control the will of the desert creatures. They dug out a mini city under the ruins of Ubar, with a specific chamber that they set the meteorite up in. Over time, they formed their own religious sect, knowing that whatever was in the meteorite was not God, but something else entirely. As far as we can tell from the translations, they call it their 'Lord'. It even mutated their animals, growing them to immense sizes, and gave them instructions – that they must protect the secret of *Ubar* forever."

Stanley snorted. "What rot."

"After all we've seen," Race said, "I am inclined to believe in some of it. This is where the survivors camped as they dug out the tunnels. That's why there is so much writing on the walls. It is a record of the fall of *Ubar* and the rise of something else, a new city built underground with the express purpose of pleasing an otherworldly Lord."

"So, what, they just let us learn all this stuff?" Jaq said.

Race looked around, suddenly wary. "I… didn't think of that."

Jaq sighed. "You don't think when you're excited, do you Doc? All of this is a trap, right down to the nice raging fire that they set for us so that we could read what was on the walls."

"How do you know?" Stanley asked.

"Because they can see in the dark."

The same unease that had been eating at Jaq's insides now gripped everyone. Race's hand went to the hilt of his sword, and he stuffed his notebook in his pocket. His mouth was suddenly bone dry, the fear seemingly flying at him from out of the darkness of the tunnels to wrap its arms around him.

Their nostrils prickled as the stench seemed to get worse. It was the sickly-sweet smell of rot that clogged their noses, threatening to make them gag. Even the fire behind them seemed to dim as the darkness crept ever closer.

"Well," Jaq said, raising her weapon to her shoulder, "let's see what they've got for us, shall we?"

CHAPTER 28

They set off, grudgingly leaving the perceived safety and warmth of the fire behind as they headed towards the tunnel that they hadn't been down yet. Jaq took the lead with her Tommy Gun, Race sticking close beside her so that he could light the way forward.

It wasn't long before they passed the passageway that led to the exit and were walking into uncharted territory, the smell getting worse with each step. It was also deathly quiet, and Race felt as if the walls around him were closing in. He found himself wishing for danger to appear so that the tension would finally break.

To Race's surprise, the tunnel they were in started to widen after a few more feet, and it only took another forty steps before the light from the party's torches no longer touched the ceiling or the walls. Only then did the Doctor realise that they had been walking down a gentle incline this whole time.

Jaq stopped suddenly, and Race almost ran into her. She put a finger to her lips before pointing to her ears. Race didn't move, straining his ears to hear what she had heard. He did.

It was faint, but it was there, the sound of something scuttling across the stone floor. And it sounded big. Massive even. Race felt the image of claws on a tiled floor come unbidden to his mind, a picture that quickened his already fast-beating heart.

"Get in a circle, lights and guns aimed out," Jaq whispered.

The party arranged themselves in a rough circle, Alsop in the middle as he was still unarmed. They pointed their torches into the dark, pushing them as far forward as they would go in an attempt to make the light stretch further. The scuttling continued, and it became clear that there was more than one colossal creature out there.

That's when the laughter started, as the party huddled together in fear in the dark. It echoed off the walls, bouncing back at them from every direction, coming from everywhere and nowhere at once.

"You are not the first foreign invaders we have had to deal with!" Said the voice in the blackness. "There have been many more before you, even white men. And they have all met the same fate."

"Show yourself, you brute!" Stanley roared.

Jaq shushed him, doing her best to discover where the man was speaking from. Laughter was the answer to Stanley's threat, a cold, dark laugh that filled everyone with dread.

"I see the English Colonel is much like any other we have seen. A coward hiding behind bluster. A man who will die begging for his life."

Jaq's hand pre-emptively grabbed the Colonel by the shoulder to stop him replying or worse, running out to meet their foe. The scuttling had stopped, giving her the sinking feeling that they were surrounded.

"I request audience with your Lord!" Race shouted suddenly.

The silence was deafening and oppressive, seeming to close in around them as Race's words echoed off the walls and then died to nothing. Undeterred, the Doctor continued.

"You have shown us so much of your history. Of your world! At least let us see the one who gave you these incredible gifts."

"Are you bargaining for your life?" Karim replied.

"No. You are going to kill us anyway, so what difference does an audience make?"

"He's right," Alsop chimed in, "what difference does it make whether we die now or later? We want to see what great and powerful being has created this kingdom, for there would be no greater honour than that."

"What makes you think you can comprehend the majesty of our Lord and Master?" Karim said.

"We did not ask to comprehend, just to be able to see Him before we die. Surely, we have earned that much after such trials?"

No reply came for a minute, during which the party kept their fingers near their triggers, anxiously waiting for creatures to leap out of the darkness and rip out their throats. Until, as Race was beginning to think that he would die of heart failure before any of the fighting started, a spark of light appeared not five feet from the party.

A torch had just been lit, the orange flame brilliant and blinding compared to the dim glow of the party's flashlights. As their eyes adjusted, they saw that the torch was being carried by the tall man in the robes. The leader of the men with the black eyes, Karim.

"You will follow me, for my Lord has granted you an audience," he said.

Race could tell that the man was not happy with this outcome. His face almost betrayed no emotion, but the tightness of his features and the stiff way in which he spoke belied his anger and frustration at not being able to kill the intruders.

Alsop shouldered his way past Jaq.

"Thank you," he said, bowing. "This is a great honour."

Karim did not reply, instead turning on his heel and striding away. Alsop walked after him, and after a brief second of indecision, so did everyone else. Around them, they could hear the clicking of claws as whatever creatures were there repositioned themselves, possibly out of frustration at being cheated out of an easy meal.

The party were led through more tunnels, Jaq taking careful note of the direction, turns, and side passages they took as they went. Race kept his grip on his sword tight, yet still managed to marvel at the passageways they were walking down, some of which were filled with carved script, others looking as if they served as living quarters, others still appearing as vast stretches of darkness that Race could not see into. The people of *Ubar* had established an underground maze as their new city.

Worryingly, some of the side passages that they passed emitted sounds of life. The scuttling of legs or the sound of creatures breathing could be heard, but the torch carried by Karim was too weak to show what was making the noises, and no one wanted to ask the man any questions, lest he decide to just kill them outright.

Finally, they arrived at a door that had been set into the rock. It was covered in a strange, arcane script that even Race did not recognise, the characters seeming ancient, even in comparison to Safaitic. The scientist within the Doctor wished that he had time to study it, but Karim had other ideas. He stopped, gave the party one last withering glare, then flung open the door to reveal a sight of such wonder that even the danger they were in was temporarily forgotten.

CHAPTER 29

The chamber beyond was massive, seemingly hundreds of meters high and equally wide. It was illuminated by a strange, alien glow that was bright enough to reach the ceiling above and the corners of the space, revealing more treasure than any man alive had ever seen.

Gold was piled so high that mounds of it was taller than three people. Statues of exquisite craftsmanship stood here and there, all from differing periods and cultures, some cast from bronze and others carved from marble. There was jewellery too, including crowns and necklaces and rings, some set with the most stunning rubies, emeralds, and diamonds, of which there were many more scattered around.

There wasn't just treasure either. Bodies in various states of decay were scattered around the area too, some in modern dress, others just skeletons or dried up husks wearing armour from various cultures and empires long since dead. Close to the entrance and to their left, Jaq noticed three dead men wearing British Army uniforms.

It all shone in the pale glow of the chamber's centrepiece – a massive chunk of meteorite whose top almost scraped the ceiling. It was set on a clear space of rock that was a foot higher than the rest of the floor, and sat leaning at an odd angle, dwarfing everything else around it.

"There's artefacts here from all over the world," Race breathed.

Karim smiled, his chest swelling with pride. "Many have tried to invade us. We have taken their treasure for our Lord to show them that we are the true rulers of this land."

"You must have been doing this for centuries."

Race saw that there was everything from modern money to ancient Roman coins around them to the skeletons of ancient Greek warriors, still clad in their helmets and breastplates. He just wanted to drop to his knees and sift through the piles of archaeological treasure, searching for anything that would give insights into the past.

Alsop hadn't stopped at the entrance with the rest of them. Instead, he had kept moving forwards and was standing at the foot of the meteorite, gazing up at it with the oddest smile on his face. His long fingers reached out to touch the surface of the thing, causing Karim to start.

"No!" He yelled. "You shall not defile our Lord!"

The reporter spun and fixed the man with such a glare that Race's blood ran cold. There seemed to be nothing good in Alsop's eyes at all, not even a trace of humanity. Just a mad lust and burning passion for destruction.

"Your Lord can speak for himself, can he not?" His eyes fixed on Karim.

Karim's rage faltered in the fury of the man's gaze. He opened his mouth, seemingly at a loss for words, then found his tongue.

"He is speaking to you, you worthless dog!" He said.

The sentence came out not with fury or bluster, but with a feeble tone, as if Alsop's gaze had truly shaken him to his heart. The reporter laughed. Karim turned to the others with wide eyes.

"Can you not hear his words?" He shouted. "He speaks to us even now!"

There was an awkward silence as everyone strained to hear something. Anything. There was nothing, however, just the crackling of the torch in the man's hand. It was broken when Alsop laughed, the sound echoing off the chamber walls, making it seem as if a hundred men were laughing with him.

"You and your men are mad, Karim," Alsop said. "This thing does not speak, for it is just a thing. A powerful thing, granted, but it cannot talk."

"What are you talking about?"

Alsop grinned. "It's such a shame when such power falls into the hands of those too stupid and too mad to use it to its fullest potential."

"Who are you?" Race asked.

Jaq had noticed something amongst the bodies of the British soldiers and was inching closer to them. Abdulrahman saw what she was up to and moved to block her from Karim's view.

"I am nobody," Alsop replied, "but I represent powerful people. People that are willing to go to the ends of the earth for artefacts such as these!"

He pointed to the meteor as he spoke, the glow from it bathing him in incandescent light and making him look like a ghoul from a horror picture.

"Shut your mouth or I shall shut it for you," Karim snarled.

"Be quiet, you fool. You've had this for centuries and all you've done is gone mad and amassed a fortune? When you could have conquered the world?"

"Our Lord just wished–"

"You have no Lord!" Alsop snapped.

Race caught sight of Jaq crouching next to one of the bodies lying on a pile of gold to the side. He stepped forward, drawing his sword, and pointing it towards Alsop.

"Who do you work for?" He asked.

The man's gaze shifted from the furious Karim to the Doctor and his weapon. A bark of derisive laughter left the reporter's throat.

"There is a man in Germany who could use this," he said. "He has plans for the world that power like this will be invaluable for. You cannot stop me, Richard, any more than this fool and his little army can."

"You're just one man, Alsop."

"Am I?"

As if on cue, gunfire erupted from the tunnels behind them. Shouts and screams of men in battle came through the passages towards them. Karim spun around to glare down the passage, then turned back to Alsop, baring his teeth and snarling like an animal.

"I will kill you, you blasphemous dog!" He said.

In one smooth movement, Alsop drew a Luger Pistol from his waistband and shot Karim in the head. The man's skull whipped backwards in a spray of gore, and he fell to the floor like a sandbag.

"No, you won't," Alsop said.

He continued to fire, pumping Karim's body full of lead, until his firing pin clicked on an empty chamber. Alsop ejected the spent magazine and slid a fresh one into the pistol with the practiced ease of a professional.

"Bloody hell," Race breathed.

"He was getting on my last nerve," Alsop said.

The sounds of battle still emanated from the tunnels behind them. It was more than men and guns too. There were inhuman screams, hisses, and other unearthly sounds.

"We need to go. Now!" Jaq said.

She was standing now, a khaki satchel slung crossways over her body, her Tommy Gun in one hand and something else in the other. Race gasped when he saw what it was. Abdulrahman had bent and picked up Karim's still-blazing torch while no one was looking.

"Bloody good idea," Stanley agreed. "Sorry about this, old chap, but you're obviously a loon!"

Jaq didn't say anything. Instead, she used the torch to light the fuse on the bundle of dynamite in her hand and tossed it towards the meteorite. Alsop's eyes widened in horror as he saw what was sailing towards him. The last thing Race saw as Jaq shoved him back outside the massive chamber and slammed the door shut was Alsop diving sideways.

"Get down!" Abdulrahman screamed.

Everyone dove to the side, away from the door, as dynamite detonated. The tunnel shook with the force of the explosion and dust rained from the ceiling as the door blew off its hinges and flew down the passage, forced outwards by a brilliant display of heat and brilliant orange flame.

CHAPTER 30

Race's ears were ringing. His back felt scorched, and his nose and throat were clogged with dust. The world was twisting and turning in odd ways, making him feel as if he was on a ship on a stormy sea, his legs acting like rubber beneath him. A sharp stinging sensation on his cheek made him start. A second later it came again, this time on the other cheek.

"Get up, you dammed limey!"

The Doctor blinked several times, and his vision cleared enough to see Jaq's face and the blur of her hand as she slapped him again.

"We need to move!" She yelled.

"I'm okay," he said, struggling to his feet, "I'm okay."

"Of course he is, he's an Englishman," Stanley said.

"Then you better bloody act like one, you hear? We got a hell of a fight before us."

As if to illustrate her point, another explosion shook the floor beneath their feet. Race stood up, using his sword as a makeshift cane to steady him. Jaq nodded, checked her newly acquired satchel, and then finally, her gun.

"We got two bundles left," she said, "and what sounds like a war between us and the exit. Stay low, move when I move, stop when I stop, and kill as many of the bastards as you can. You all got that?"

Stanley racked the bolt of his rifle.

"Yes, ma'am," he said, then turned to Race and added, "never thought I'd take orders from a bloody yank."

They followed Jaq as she took off at a jog, Race once-again lighting the way with his flashlight, Stanley in the middle, and Abdulrahman bringing up the rear with Karim's torch in his hands.

As they moved, they could hear the battle getting closer. Visions of the trenches flashed through Race's mind when the familiar smells of war hit his nostrils. It was all too familiar, and he felt his stomach lurch. He'd vowed never to walk into a hell like it again, yet it seemed that fate had other plans.

A glance over to Jaq showed a look of grim determination on her face. It was an expression of such focus, such confidence, that it gave Race some hope that they might survive. A hope that was soon faltering in his breast as they came upon the massive cavern where they had met Karim earlier.

It was like a scene from Dante's hell. Lit by flames and the staccato flashes of gunfire, man and beast were fighting to the death in a scene so absurd that none of the party would have believed it had it not been in front of them.

High above, monstrously large bats flew with their riders, swooping down to swipe, claw, and slash at the troops on the ground. Giant serpents weaved in and out of the crowd of men, one of which clasped a man between its jaws and tossed him across the cavern. And then there were the scorpions – colossal beasts being ridden by men, their tails implausibly fast and stings deathly accurate.

But the battle was not one-sided. The men who Jaq assumed were Alsop's had come prepared. All were equipped with the German-made Erma EMP submachine gun, a weapon with a 32-round magazine, a fire rate of 550 rpm, and an effective killing range of 150 meters. The constant barrage of automatic fire played hard on everyone's eardrums. It was evident that they were also using explosives, as the beaten and blazing bodies of the scorpions and snakes could attest, and one man was using a flamethrower, sending great jets of brilliant orange flame towards the serpents and scorpions around him.

"It's a bloody invasion," Stanley said.

As they watched, one of the mercenaries was picked up by the pincer of one of the scorpions. He screamed an almost-inhuman cry of pain as he was raised in the air, one hand digging something out of his khaki combat fatigues as he went. A second later, the man was replaced by a ball of fire and heat as he detonated an explosive, obliterating half of the scorpion. The creature screamed in pain and thrashed its stumps, spraying gooey fluid around the battlefield.

Dust fell from above as the shockwave from the explosion reached the walls. Two immense pieces of stone fell from above, one of them hitting a bat and its rider on the way down and sending them tumbling towards the floor with an ear-splitting screech.

"If we don't move soon, then this cavern will bury us," Abdulrahman observed.

Jaq nodded, surveying the scene, looking for any route through the carnage that might offer a reasonable chance of survival. Then their time ran out.

Attracted by the glow of their torches, a bat rider swung his beast in their direction, shouting to his fellows. Worse still, a scorpion turned its massive carapace towards them, its rider issued a command, and the great arachnid started its charge, Jaq, Race, and the other two set firmly in its beady sights.

CHAPTER 31

Jaq reacted first, raising her weapon to her shoulder and letting loose a burst of fire that tore into the scorpion's rider. The man bucked in his seat, blood spurting forth from his chest like a gory fountain, and he fell sideways. His beast kept coming, however, forcing Jaq to lower her aim towards the thing's head.

Meanwhile, Stanley and Abdulrahman took aim at the bats that were tearing through the air towards them. Abdulrahman was the best shot among the two of them, taking down two of the four beasts with headshots that dropped them from the sky. Stanley was less lucky, only getting one of the bats, forcing the two of them to dive sideways as the one remaining creature's rider slashed at them from above.

The rider was surprised to find his slash deflected by Race, the unexpected obstacle of another sword throwing him off-balance and forcing him to pull on the reigns of his mount. The bat responded by jerking sideways suddenly, sending both it and its rider careening into the darkness.

Jaq's bullets weren't penetrating the scorpion's tough hide, which may as well have been made of solid steel. It twitched as the rounds ricocheted off it, but kept coming, seemingly more determined to skewer its prey with its stinger.

As the thing bore down on her, Jaq dropped to a knee, and took careful aim at the creature's eyes – two black gleaming dots atop the thing's head. Ignoring how fast the deadly monster was closing the distance, she took a breath, took aim, and squeezed the trigger on the exhale.

A barrage of .45 ACP rounds were sent hurtling towards the scorpion's eyes at 935 feet per second, hitting their mark just as the arachnid got within stinging distance of the crouched Jaq. As its tail was about to come down, it abruptly found itself blinded, and it reacted as any animal would – by panicking. It screeched and thrashed, forcing Jaq to roll backwards as the thing came within a hair's breadth of stomping her to death.

Race saw the creature thrashing around and took his chance. He rushed up behind it and slashed at its tail with his sword, the strange, alien metal of the blade slicing through the hard outer shell of the beast almost effortlessly. He then kicked it in the head with his foot, sending the animal scuttling back into the heat of battle.

Another explosion rocked the cavern as Race helped Jaq to her feet. They nodded to each other, cast a glance at the Colonel and Abdulrahman, and discovered that they too were ready to move.

"Only one way out," Race said.

Jaq dropped her expended magazine and shoved a fresh drum into her weapon, her second-last.

"Through em," she said.

Jaq covered left, Race right, with Abdulrahman and Stanley keeping their rear and flank under guard as they chose a path to take through the chaos and charged towards it. Jaq fired in short, sharp bursts, cutting down man and beast, while Race slashed this way and that with his sword. Behind, the Colonel and Abdulrahman fought side-by-side, the bang, clack, bang of their rifles firing and cocking forming a strange rhythm.

Cordite, the copper scent of blood, the stench of entrails, and the smell of burning flesh – both human and not – choked them as they charged into the fray. Somehow, the screams and cries of the dying could still be heard over the roar of war, not to mention the calls of the animals. And it seemed as if Karim's men, with their beastly companions and bizarre capacity to withstand pain, were gaining the upper hand.

As Jaq slammed her last magazine into her Tommy Gun, she saw that another wave of attackers had singled the party out. Two scorpions and a snake were heading their way, closing the distance so fast that she barely had time to shout a warning.

Race saw them coming too. He turned his attention to the snake as it struck, ducking and slashing upwards with his sword. The weapon cut into the throat of the beast, its fangs tearing through the Doctor's shirt, but thankfully just missing his skin. Blood rained down upon him in a crimson waterfall as the thing died.

Jaq didn't even bother with the Thompson, instead throwing herself backwards while simultaneously scrabbling for another bundle of dynamite in the satchel.

Abdulrahman was too concentrated on other enemies at eight o'clock to notice the two arachnids coming towards him. Stanley did see them, but his rifle had just clicked empty as he did so.

Seeing the things about to kill his friend, he let out a bellow, threw his useless rifle at one of the creatures and drew down on the other with his Webley. In less than two seconds, he had pumped five rounds into the scorpion on the right, blinding it just as Jaq had with the other one, causing its rider to struggle to control the thrashing creature. But the one on the left shrugged off the thrown rifle and struck with its stinger.

A pain unlike any other shot through Colonel Stanley's body. Unbearably hot, it lanced throughout his nerves like wildfire, and he screamed a tortured cry of unimaginable agony. Then he was being pulled sideways, someone yelling something incomprehensible at him.

Race had cut through the scorpion's tail just a split-second too late. The thing had already pierced Stanley in the back. Grasping the stinger and wrenching it out of the

Colonel's body, he pushed the man with the other hand, urging him to move as Jaq lit the bundle of dynamite, which she tossed almost immediately.

The Doctor saw it sail overhead as Abdulrahman grabbed him and Stanley and pulled them to the ground. The explosives landed between the two scorpions, who were still flailing in pain, and their riders realised what the bundle was just before it detonated, obliterating them and half their arachnid mounts in a ball of fire and fury. The beasts collapsed into a heap of translucent, burbling arachnid goo and guts.

There was no time to rest, as bullets screamed past overhead, and more creatures turned their attention to the group.

"Help me!" Race called.

He was trying to lift Stanley, who was drooling on himself and mumbling. Abdulrahman came to their aid, helping Race to heft the Colonel up between them. Jaq was already on her feet, letting loose with the Thompson at a group of bats above. The creatures screeched and scattered, throwing off their riders and flying away in terror as hot lead tore through the air around them.

The group pushed onwards, Jaq providing covering fire as they made their way towards the exit. Around them, the battle was dying down as Karim's men gained the upper hand. Men were being skewered by scorpions, having their heads lopped off by flying enemies, and being injected with litres of toxic snake venom. Their deaths were horrific, and Race felt bile rise in his throat from both fear and revulsion.

Jaq's Thompson ran dry, and she tossed the weapon to the side. She bent to scoop up an EMP submachine gun from a dead man's hands, hoping desperately that it had bullets in it. She had her answer when she raised it to fire at a bat as it swooped towards her, its rider's sword glinting in the light of a nearby fire.

The weapon bucked in her hands and the rider fell from his mount, dead. She thanked whatever Gods there were as she kept going, keeping her pace as fast as she could without leaving the other three behind.

Abdulrahman was holding Stanley up with one arm while firing his Webley revolver with the other. He was doing his best to make the six round cylinder last, picking his shots carefully. He put a bullet in the head of a man who attempted to bring his EMP to bear on them and sent two rounds towards the eyes of a riderless scorpion just in time to stop it from charging.

The whole cavern was shaking. Dust was raining down from the ceiling, along with rocks of varying sizes. The smartest of the combatants had realised what was happening and had abandoned the fight to head for the exit. Some didn't even make it more than a few steps before being crushed by falling stone.

A bullet caught the fuel cannister of the flamethrower and the thing exploded in a great big ball of fire, the searing heat riding through the air and touching Jaq's face as she ran. Thick black smoke washed through the cavern, as if from the very pits of hell itself.

A great, zig-zagging crack tore its way along the ground barely three feet from her boots. It started to grow wider and wider, and she watched as a scorpion and its rider fell into the chasm. Both screamed as they tumbled into the abyss.

"Fuck, fuck, fuck," Jaq said.

She discarded the empty submachine gun so that she could draw her Colt. Behind her, Race and Abdulrahman were having trouble with the Colonel. His legs had entirely given out and hung uselessly, his boots dragging along the ground as the two men carried him forward.

The exit was tantalisingly close. Jaq risked a glance over her shoulder and gasped at the site of the entire cavern caving in, all while a massive crevasse opened in the middle of it. Men were screaming and running about in panic. Karim's men had all lost control of their mounts, which had sensed what was going on and succumbed to blind, instinctive terror.

Jaq tore her gaze away from the pandemonium, instead focusing on getting to the tunnel that would lead them up to the surface.

The gunfire had ceased, replaced by the cracking and crumbling of rock. The ground still shook and the few still alive found it hard to maintain their balance.

Still, the group pushed on. Abdulrahman and Race were struggling as every muscle in their body screamed at them to stop and their lungs burned hotter than the fires of hell. But they could see the exit.

Finally, Jaq crossed into the shelter of the escape tunnel, the other three just a second behind. Yet the destruction was still coming, the massive canyon widening and heading straight for them. She pushed the three men ahead of her, yelling at them to keep going, hoping against hope that the exit hadn't been sealed.

The trek became harder as they now had to drag Stanley uphill. They weren't going to make it. They were too slow.

Race screamed at Jaq to go ahead. That at least she could make it.

But she refused, instead doing her best to push them forward.

Then Stanley came too and using his last few moments of clarity as the poison coursed through his body, shrugged out of the grip of his fellows. Race turned to him, aghast, as the Colonel smiled and raised his Webley to his head.

"For King and country," he said.

Then he used his last bullet to shoot himself.

Jaq saw it happen and was the first to recognise the man's sacrifice, so she picked up the pace, pushing the stunned Race and Abdulrahman to run. Their instincts took over even if their minds did not comprehend what was going on and all three of them took off at a sprint, expending the last of their failing energy in the desperate rush to survive.

The roar was all-consuming now, seeming to come from everywhere, even inside their own bodies. They could hear nothing but grinding stone and trembling earth – not even their own petrified and fraught screams.

Then, finally, using the last ounce of strength left in their bodies, they flung themselves out into the cool, moonlit night as the passageway collapsed behind them in a cloud of dust.

CHAPTER 32

The three of them lay in the soft, still hot sand, coughing and spluttering as the swirling dust cloud washed over them. Jaq squinted through tearing eyes to see the most beautiful thing she had ever seen – the stars in the clear, black sky. Beside her, Abdulrahman was offering a prayer to *Allah*, and Race was giggling like a mad schoolboy, until the thought of Stanley's death sobered him.

Jaq raised herself to her knees, looking up to see the barrel of an EMP pointing at her head. Beyond it was the stern, heavily lined face of a grey-haired man in khaki fatigues of the kind worn by the mercenaries that had presumably all perished in the cavern. Behind him stood three other men, all similarly dressed and armed.

"No sudden moves," the man said.

His accent was definitely German, although Jaq could not place which part of Germany he came from. His eyes were a most brilliant shade of blue and they were locked on her hand. The one that held the Colt .45.

"Stand up slowly, all of you," the man demanded. "Hands above your head. And leave the weapon on the ground, please, Miss Van Alden."

Jaq, Race, and Abdulrahman stood on jelly-like legs that wobbled slightly as they struggled to remain upright. Race tried to hold his hands up, but after carrying the Colonel for so long, realised that they were too weak for that, so dropped them to his side.

"Shoot me if you want, you bastards," he said, spitting a gob of phlegm onto the ground by the grey-haired man's feet, "but I'm too bloody tired to keep my hands up."

"Where is Alsop?" The man asked.

"Dead, hopefully," Jaq replied.

"A pity. What about the artefact?"

"Buried with Alsop under about a thousand tons of rock and sand, pilgrim. See for yourself."

She stepped to the side to show the man the tunnel. Or rather, to show him where the tunnel used to be. The man swore.

"So, we have come all this way for nothing," he said. "Too bad. This means that you three shall have to die."

"Yeah, I kind of figured that," Jaq said.

The man smirked. "Any last words?"

"Yeah. On behalf of the United States of America, go fu–"

Something exploded out of the ground just below the feet of grey-haired man's comrades, sending them soaring into the air in a cloud of dust and debris. The man turned to see what had happened, only for a scorpion stinger to dash forth from the dust and impale him through the abdomen. His finger twitched in a death grip on the trigger of his weapon, sending a spray of bullets into the dirt and Jaq and the others leaping for cover, as the creature lifted him high into the air, then with a flick of its tail, sent the body flying into the distance.

As the dust settled, Jaq was horrified to see not just a monstrous arachnid, but something even more terrifying. It had the body of a scorpion, but it had somehow fused into the torsos of both Alsop and Karim, who had themselves blended into a grisly two-headed facsimile of a person. Their flesh had morphed and melted together, leaving an obvious seam, and embedded in the flesh of the ghastly creature were bits and pieces of the meteorite that still glowed.

The two heads of the gruesome monstrosity turned towards Jaq as one and a grin spread over their features.

"Hello, Miss Van Alden," the thing said, the two voices as melded as the body it spoke from.

"Bloody hell," Race said.

"It appears that you did me a favour by blowing us to pieces, Jaq," the creature said. "I have never felt so good. Having eight legs is a lot better than just two. And these pincers are, quite frankly, invaluable."

In demonstration, the Alsop-scorpion flicked out a pincer and snatched up one of the men who had been rising to his feet. With a click, it snapped the thing closed on the unfortunate man and he was cut in half with a wet, mushy sound resembling pudding falling to the floor.

"See?"

The monster laughed. As it did, Jaq snatched up her weapon and pumped seven .45 calibre rounds into the thing's two heads.

It did not even blink, the smile not once leaving its horribly contorted features.

"Did you really think that would work?" It asked.

"I was hoping," Jaq admitted.

She was trying to think of what to do when Race charged past her with his sword held high.

"Run!" He screamed as he thrust the weapon down into the chest of the human part of the Alsop-scorpion.

The blade embedded itself into the surprisingly malleable flesh with ease and the point came out the other side. The thing laughed, and with a flick of its pincer, sent Race sailing through the air. Before the Doctor had even landed, its eyes landed on Jaq and Abdulrahman. Its tongue darted out of its mouth to lick its pallid lips.

While Race had been stabbing the thing, Jaq had reloaded, and she opened fire once more, using it as a distraction while she backed up. Abdulrahman grabbed her by the shoulders and pulled her along, the two of them breaking into a sprint. The Alsop-scorpion laughed, watching as they ran. It was about to give chase when bullets slammed into it from behind.

The two horrified mercenaries who had been standing behind the grey haired man watched as the creature turned its gaze towards them, their barrage of gunfire seeming to have no effect. Before they could blink, the tail had flicked out twice, delivering a lethal dose of poison that killed them both in less than a second.

With a twisted human hand made up of two arms and ten fingers, the Alsop-scorpion reached up and pulled the sword out of its chest. It tossed it into the ruins of the city, laughing as it landed with a clatter.

"I'm coming for you, Jaqueline Van Alden!" It said.

Jaq and Abdulrahman were running, dodging this way and that through the sand-blasted ruins of *Ubar*. They skidded to a halt near a partially ruined building and pressed themselves up against the crumbling wall, panting.

"How do we kill that?" Jaq asked.

"The dynamite is our only hope," Abdulrahman said.

Behind them, they could hear the click-clacking of the Alsop-scorpion's many legs as it climbed over the remnants of the once-mighty city that it had played a part in destroying.

"This is my city," said its weird two-person voice, "I claimed it for my own many years ago. And I shall do so again, after I rip you two to shreds."

Jaq searched her pockets, hoping to find her lighter. She looked at Abdulrahman in despair. He delved into his own and pulled out a silver lighter with as much of a flourish as he could manage, considering the situation.

Jaq was about to grab it when the wall they were leaning against exploded towards them. The Alsop-scorpion had used one of its pincers to smash through it, sending Jaq flying to the left and Abdulrahman tumbling to the right. The thing let out a shriek of laughter that sounded more bestial than human.

Abdulrahman scrambled backwards just in time to avoid the stinger of the scorpion as it landed in the dirt. He watched as the tail raised to strike once more, frantically trying to get up and start running, his legs not co-operating, his own body telling him that he was done. That there would be no more running.

As the tail reached its peak, and the Alsop-scorpion laughed its inhuman laugh, Jaq came up behind it with the sword and slashed at the thing's tail. She used every ounce of her strength, putting her hips into the swing like she was swinging a baseball bat at a ball.

It wasn't enough.

The sword embedded itself in the creature's tail, its armour seemingly a lot tougher now that it had fused with the meteorite. Jaq backed away as the Alsop-scorpion turned to face her, leaving the sword where it was. She pulled the dynamite bundle out of the satchel and held it high, causing the creature to hesitate.

"You think that'll kill me?" It asked.

"I can try," Jaq said.

Behind the monster, Abdulrahman staggered to his feet and threw the lighter with every ounce of strength he had left in his body. It sailed through the air, arcing towards Jaq's outstretched hand, and she would have caught it had one of the Alsop-scorpion's ten-fingered hands not shot out and snatched it from the air in a split-second.

The Alsop-scorpion looked at the silver lighter in his hand, then to Jaq's crestfallen face. It laughed again, smiling its ghastly grin.

"No last second save for you, I'm afraid, Miss Van Alden."

"Jaq throw it!" Came Race's sudden shout.

Jaq didn't hesitate. She tossed the dynamite at the creature and dove backwards as it caught it absentmindedly in its free hand, before turning to face Race.

Doctor Richard Race stood with his feet set, and a heavy four-foot vertical cylinder on his back that had been split in two from top to bottom. In his hands was a rubber tube that ended in a steel nozzle, the opening of which was pointed directly at the Alsop-scorpion.

"You always were a wanker, Alsop," Race said and depressed the lever.

A jet of bright orange flame shot forth from the nozzle of the flamethrower, igniting the Alsop-creature. Its flesh caught like cheap polyester, and the entire creature was ablaze in seconds. It screamed in pain, a cry so loud and so shrill that Race's ears bled. But the scream was cut short when the flames touched the dynamite.

There was a flash and a whump as the explosives ignited, sucking all the oxygen out of the air in a second, consuming the flaming monster that had once been two men and a giant scorpion. The shockwave knocked Race off his feet and the huge boom echoed across the desert for miles.

CHAPTER 33

Charred, smoking pieces of what was the Alsop-scorpion rained down around Jaq like the hail of the damned, and all she could do was smile. She sat up and was about to call to Abdulrahman when he offered his hand to her.

"You okay, Jaq?" He asked, pulling her to her feet.

The stench of overdone BBQ made her choke, but she managed a nod.

"Never better. Race?"

"I'm okay!" Race called. "I just need some help, is all."

They found him on his back, his arms and legs in the air like some bizarre turtle, unable to extricate himself from the heavy flamethrower. Once they had managed to get him out of the device and back on his feet, they surveyed the damage.

"Where'd you get that thing?" Jaq asked.

"Alsop's people came prepared," he said. "There's a whole mess of supplies in one of the huts nearby. Camels too. There was one guard with a lit flamethrower, but he dropped it and ran once he heard the creature."

"Are there enough supplies to get us home?" Abdulrahman said.

He toed a piece of Alsop-scorpion flesh with his boot. It squelched unpleasantly.

"Oh yes. They brought enough for their little army. All those sketches Alsop was working on? He was leaving them at our campsites. It wasn't just pictures; it was maps too. They must have been following us the whole time."

"I don't think we need to worry about them anymore," Jaq said, glancing at the filled-in tunnel.

"What do we say about what happened to us on this expedition?"

"I think, Doctor Race," Jaq said, "that we just tell them we couldn't find The Atlantis of the Sands."

A piece of Alsop-scorpion flesh fell from atop a nearby wall, landing in the sand with a wet squelch.

"That would be best."

"Of course," Abdulrahman said, "we could always come back for all that treasure sometime."

Jaq smiled. "Now, there's an idea."

THE END

🐦 @severedpress
f /severedpress

Check out other great
Cryptid Novels!

P.K. Hawkins
THE CRYPTID FILES

Fresh out of the academy with top marks, Agent Bradley Tennyson is expecting to have the pick of cases and investigations throughout the country. So he's shocked when instead he is assigned as the new partner to "The Crag," an agent well past his prime. He thinks the assignment is a punishment. It's anything but.Agent George Crag has been doing this job for far longer than most, and he knows what skeletons his bosses have in the closet and where the bodies are buried. He has pretty much free reign to pick his cases, and he knows exactly which one he wants to use to break in his new young partner: the disappearance and murder of a couple of college kids in a remote mountain town.Tennyson doesn't realize it, but Crag is about to introduce him to a world he never believed existed: The Cryptid Files, a world of strange monsters roaming in the night. Because these murders have been going on for a long time, and evidence is mounting that the murderer may just in fact be the legendary Bigfoot.

Gerry Griffiths
DOWN FROM BEAST MOUNTAIN

A beast with a grudge has come down from the mountain to terrorize the townsfolk of Porterville. The once sleepy town is suddenly wide awake. Sheriff Abel McGuire and game warden Grant Tanner frantically investigate one brutal slaying after another as they follow the blood trail they hope will eventually lead to the monstrous killer. But they better hurry and stop the carnage before the census taker has to come out and change the population sign on the edge of town to ZERO.

Check out other great
Cryptid Novels!

J.H. Moncrieff
RETURN TO DYATLOV PASS

In 1959, nine Russian students set off on a skiing expedition in the Ural Mountains. Their mutilated bodies were discovered weeks later. Their bizarre and unexplained deaths are one of the most enduring true mysteries of our time. Nearly sixty years later, podcast host Nat McPherson ventures into the same mountains with her team, determined to finally solve the mystery of the Dyatlov Pass incident. Her plans are thwarted on the first night, when two trackers from her group are brutally slaughtered. The team's guide, a superstitious man from a neighboring village, blames the killings on yetis, but no one believes him. As members of Nat's team die one by one, she must figure out if there's a murderer in their midst—or something even worse—before history repeats itself and her group becomes another casualty of the infamous Dead Mountain.

Gerry Griffiths
CRYPTID ZOO

As a child, rare and unusual animals, especially cryptid creatures, always fascinated Carter Wilde. Now that he's an eccentric billionaire and runs the largest conglomerate of high-tech companies all over the world, he can finally achieve his wildest dream of building the most incredible theme park ever conceived on the planet... CRYPTID ZOO. Even though there have been apparent problems with the project, Wilde still decides to send some of his marketing employees and their families on a forced vacation to assess the theme park in preparation for Opening Day. Nick Wells and his family are some of those chosen and are about to embark on what will become the most terror-filled weekend of their lives—praying they survive. STEP RIGHT UP AND GET YOUR FREE PASS... TO CRYPTID ZOO

Check out other great

Cryptid Novels!

Hunter Shea

LOCH NESS REVENGE

Deep in the murky waters of Loch Ness, the creature known as Nessie has returned. Twins Natalie and Austin McQueen watched in horror as their parents were devoured by the world's most infamous lake monster. Two decades later, it's their turn to hunt the legend. But what lurks in the Loch is not what they expected. Nessie is devouring everything in and around the Loch, and it's not alone. Hell has come to the Scottish Highlands. In a fierce battle between man and monster, the world may never be the same. Praise for THEY RISE : "Outrageous, balls to the wall...made me yearn for 3D glasses and a tub of popcorn, extra butter!" – The Eyes of Madness "A fast-paced, gore-heavy splatter fest of sharksploitation." The Werd "A rocket paced horror story. I enjoyed the hell out of this book." Shotgun Logic Reviews

C.G. Mosley

BAKER COUNTY BIGFOOT CHRONICLE

Marie Bledsoe only wants her missing brother Kurt back. She'll stop at nothing to make it happen and, with the help of Kurt's friend Tony, along with Sheriff Ray Cochran, Marie embarks on a terrifying journey deep into the belly of the mysterious Walker Laboratory to find him. However, what she and her companions find lurking in the laboratory basement is beyond comprehension. There are cryptids from the forest being held captive there and something...else. Enjoy this suspenseful tale from the mind of C.G. Mosley, author of Wood Ape. Welcome back to Baker County, a place where monsters do lurk in the night!